THE
STEAM WHISTLE
THEATRE
COMPANY

THE
STEAM WHISTLE
THEATRE
COMPANY

Vivian French

**WALKER
BOOKS**

First published in Great Britain 2019 by Walker Books Ltd
87 Vauxhall Walk, London SE11 5HJ

2 4 6 8 10 9 7 5 3 1

Text © 2019 Vivian French
Cover art and illustrations by Hannah Peck

The right of Vivian French and Hannah Peck to be identified as author and illustrator respectively of this work has been asserted by them in accordance with the Copyright, Designs and Patents Act 1988

This book has been typeset in Libre Baskerville and Blackfriar

Printed and bound by CPI Group (UK) Ltd, Croydon CR0 4YY

British Library Cataloguing in Publication Data:
a catalogue record for this book is
available from the British Library

ISBN 978-1-4063-7631-9

www.walker.co.uk

For dearest Caz, with all my love

DRAMATIS PERSONAE

The Steam Whistle Theatre Company

Fred "Pa" Pringle – lead-actor and director of the company

Betty "Ma" Pringle – resides in London

Aunt Mags Pringle – actor and financial supervisor of the company; Pa's sister

Charlie Pringle – child-actor; Pa's son

Rosie Pringle – child-actor; Pa's daughter

Gertrude "Gertie" Gracegirdle – lead-singer of the company

Vincent von Greazle – actor; Gertie's husband

CITIZENS OF UNCASTER

Arabella Poskett – Lady of Uncaster Hall

Affogato Poskett – Arabella's son

Hypatia Poskett – Arabella's daughter

Edie Boiler – housemaid at Uncaster Hall

The Honourable Jocasta Poskett – Arabella's
    sister-in-law

Mrs Moore – proprietor of Mrs Moore's
    Supper Rooms

Jago – serving boy at Mrs Moore's Supper
    Rooms; aspiring actor

Mr Tramways – head of Uncaster's Post Office

Miss Twillfit – owner of the local milliners'

Ne'er-do-wells

Little Baby Bubbles – the One and Only
    Child Master of Magic and Escapology

Eliza Snicket – Baby Bubbles' mother

Olio Sleevery – a landlord of ill repute

One

"**M**URDER!" PA PRINGLE CLENCHED HIS FISTS, and scowled a terrible scowl. "Dark and deadly deeds! That'll bring 'em in!"

Aunt Mags gave a disparaging sniff. "No, Fred. I say we choose *The Sad Tale of a Long Lost Child*. Murder brings in the riff-raff, and we get those sneaky boys creeping in without paying. They don't bother when it's long lost children, or orphans."

Charlie, sitting in a corner and half-hidden by strings of washing, made a face at Rosie. "Got more sense," he whispered.

Rosie ignored her brother. Her big brown eyes and curly hair meant that she was the one chosen to play abandoned daughters, little lost heiresses or wistful orphans.

This had advantages: her parts involved wearing silk dresses or artistically designed rags, and she didn't have to learn too many lines. Wistful orphans were not usually given to long speeches. Instead, they sighed a good deal, and clasped their hands together while silver tears trickled down their pale and hollow cheeks. Rosie could cry to order, especially if she had a piece of onion hidden in her handkerchief.

Charlie came out from behind the sheets and shirts. "What about *Pirate Pete, Captain of the Saucy Skull and Scourge of the Spanish Main*, Pa? Everyone likes that!"

Pa looked thoughtful. "There's an idea. What do you think, Mags?"

"Really, Fred! You can't have forgotten!" Aunt Mags held up a reproving finger. "I told you last week. Due to our unfortunate lack of funds, Vinnie and I were forced to leave the Saucy Skull's sails and anchor at the Red Lion in lieu of payment. I said at the time it was an error of judgement. We should have left a promise to pay instead."

"We've done that too often." Pa rolled his eyes. "They know it's not worth the paper it's written on. They know us too well, if truth be told." He heaved such an enormous sigh that his many chins quivered. "It's hard times for the Pringle Players. Maybe I should give up, and get myself a little market stall." He lumbered to his feet, puffed out his chest and put his hands on his hips. *"Come along, come along, ladies and gents! Get your fresh fruit here! You never saw such rosy apples, straight from the fields of Kent! Rosy as the cheeks of your very own sweetheart! Come buy, come buy!"*

Aunt Mags was unimpressed. "No good, Fred. You'd be bored within a week, and that's a fact."

"If they know us too well here, Pa, why don't we go somewhere else?" Rosie came to stand beside her father. "What about going outside London?"

"Yes!" Charlie nodded enthusiastically. "We could go North! Bet they'd love us there. Don't suppose they've ever seen players like us!" He paused. "Do they speak English?"

"North?" Aunt Mags' tone suggested that she thoroughly disapproved of anywhere beyond Camden Town. "That's foreign. Besides, how would we get there? Hetty's old. She'd never pull the cart that far."

Pa Pringle put his hand on his heart. "And that, my dears, is the terrible truth. Our beloved four-legged friend, who has been our loyal companion for so many, many years—" He fished in his pocket, brought out a large spotty handkerchief, and wiped his eyes— "is not going to last much longer. So there we are, we're done for. The last act of the Pringle Players is staring us in the face: the curtain will fall, and we'll have to take our final bow. The lights will slowly dim..."

"TRAIN!" Rosie clapped her hands. "We could go by train! I've seen the trains, Pa – they have carts a bit like ours, but the train pulls them!"

"We could go anywhere!" Charlie's eyes were shining. "North, South, East, West – anywhere the train goes!"

"North, South, East, West..." Pa said thoughtfully. "North, South, East, West! I like the sound of that. Yes – yes, yes, YES!" He seized Charlie and Rosie, and whirled them round. "We will seize the opportunity, and live to play again!"

◆ ◆ ◆

It took the combined efforts of Pa, Charlie, and Rosie to convince Aunt Mags that travelling on a train wasn't certain death on wheels. Ma Pringle was also doubtful, but Charlie and Rosie's enthusiasm – together with the hope of a rise in income – eventually persuaded her it might be worth trying.

"After all," she said, "our dear Queen Victoria goes by train. If it's good enough for her, it should be good enough for us."

Aunt Mags sniffed. "She probably has a special carriage. Padded, I expect, so when it overturns she doesn't get hurt. Royalty live by different rules."

"If you'd come with me, Mags, you'd see for yourself." The idea of a new way of travelling had seized Pa's imagination, and he had spent the last few days visiting Victoria, Paddington, St Pancras and Kings Cross stations, studying timetables and discussing routes with anyone prepared to talk to him. "Safe as houses, trains. Bit mucky, mind, but we can pack all the props and costumes safely away."

"Horrid dirty things," Aunt Mags grumbled.

"I've seen them going along the viaduct – and I've seen what they do to the washing hanging out in the gardens down below. Disgusting! You'll never ever get me on one of those, not if the Queen herself was to beg me on her bended knees."

"Alas!" Pa Pringle slapped his head with a despairing cry. "Alas! So the Pringle Players must continue without their finest member! No more can our audiences thrill to the dulcet tones of Miss Margaretta Pringle, as she declaims the immortal words of our dearly beloved Bard. No longer can we offer that well-known tableau, the crowning of the Queen of Sheba, with accompanying song and dance." He leant against the wall, closed his eyes and sighed his most heart-rending sigh.

Rosie nudged Charlie. They knew their aunt well. "Ten!" Rosie whispered.

"Nah ... it's an eight at most," Charlie whispered back.

Together they silently counted on their fingers. "One, two, three—"

Before they had even reached six, Aunt Mags had blown her nose, taken a deep breath – and given in. "If you really think it's for the best, Fred, I'll go." Then, feeling she hadn't made enough of a dramatic moment, she flung out her arms. "Forgive me, Fred! What a miserable wretch I am, putting my own comfort before the needs of our little troupe of players. Take me to a train, and I will put my objections to one side and suffer agonies in the name of Art."

Much relieved, Pa Pringle patted his sister on the shoulder. "Well said, old girl. Trains are the way of the future, and that's what we need: a future. There's a few bills that need paying, and we owe quite a bit on the rooms here – and the family's not getting any smaller. Isn't that right, Ma?"

Ma nodded. Little Billy was on her knee, Betty and Sally-Ann were sitting on the floor at her feet, and baby Joe was tucked up in a basket by the fire. "That's very true." An anxious expression crossed her face. "You're not thinking of doing a flit, are you? That's not right, Fred! You know it's not! Mrs Dobbs, she's been good to us. She trusts us – she says she knows we'll pay her when we come into funds."

"Flit? FLIT? And leave a generous woman in

distress?" Pa did his best to sound outraged, but Charlie winked at Rosie. "Flitting. That's what he was thinking, sure as eggs is eggs."

Rosie sighed. "I hate doing that."

Charlie shrugged. "What else can we do? We can't make shillings out of pennies. Besides, Ma's got her honesty book. She writes down what we owe when we leave anywhere without settling up, so when we're rich we can pay it all back. That's almost as good as paying, isn't it? And think what a wonderful surprise it'll be when we come knocking at the door to hand over the silver! Why, they'll hardly believe their eyes!"

"Maybe." Rosie wasn't convinced.

"Come on, sis! We've got a new beginning ahead! We're going on the trains, and we'll make our fortune in no time!"

Pa Pringle heard Charlie, and he beamed from ear to ear. "That's my boy! Always looking for the sunshine! And you're right. There's a fortune out there, just waiting for the Pringle Players." He stopped, and a thoughtful expression came over his face. "Just a minute. What was it you said? A new beginning? Hmmmm ...

you're right. And it seems to me that a New Beginning should have a new name. The Pringle Players? Done for. No horse, no future. But in just a few days a new company will be taking to the rails..." Pa's voice deepened, and his chest expanded. "A company that scorns the limits of a geographical border. A company of inspiring thespians bringing stirring drama, heart-rending tragedy, and extraordinary excitement to the dull and uninformed minds that lie beyond the boundaries of the fair city of London."

Pa flung out his arms, and struck his most impressive pose.

"We, my dear family, will rise from the ashes like the – like the – like that fabulous bird of old whose name temporarily escapes me. From today, and for all time, we will be renewed."

Seizing Little Billy in his arms and tossing him onto his broad shoulders, he thundered round the room.

"All aboard! All aboard for fame and fortune! *Chuff-chuff-chuff-chuff, chuff-chuff-chuff-chuff! Wheeeeeeeeeeee!*" Pa's imitation of a train whistle was remarkably accurate; Little Billy roared with laughter and pulled Pa's hair to make him do it again. "*Wheeeeeeeeeeee! WHEEEEEEEEE!* OH!"

Pa Pringle skidded to a sudden and abrupt halt. "That's it! That's it! That's the name!" His large round face was scarlet with excitement. "We, my dears, will be the Steam Whistle Theatre Company!"

Two

FAR AWAY IN THE SMALL MARKET TOWN OF Uncaster, Mrs Arabella Poskett was staring gloomily at a pile of bills. They were not the kind of bills that enquire, politely, if the recipient would like to pay sometime in the future – entirely at their own convenience. These bills were sour, threatening and universally unpleasant. "Money, money, money. Dearest Papa never taught me how useful it could be. And poor darling Henry ... it's only too obvious that he didn't know anything about it either."

Arabella was mistaken. The Honourable Henry Poskett had had very definite views on the subject of money: he liked spending it. He liked spending it so much that his sudden death (due to a mistaken belief that he could walk round the battlements of Uncaster Hall with his hat over his eyes) had left his wife and children with nothing – or rather less than nothing, as it now appeared. Since his death, bills had arrived by every post: bills for boots, dogs, horses, champagne (none of which had been drunk by his wife), top hats, shirts, a surprising number of velvet suits, silk handkerchiefs, two silver shaving sets ... the list seemed endless.

Arabella sighed again, and moved the bills to the other side of the table in the hopes that the pile might look smaller. It didn't, and she pulled a damp lace handkerchief out of her pocket and wiped her eyes.

"Mother!" Arabella's daughter had come hurrying into the drawing room. "Mother! Cook's packed her bags, and so have all the other servants! They say they're leaving right now this minute, and they won't even make me any lunch! Go and tell them they have to!"

Arabella looked up with tear-filled eyes. "I can't, Hypatia darling. They haven't been paid, you see, and if servants aren't paid then they won't work."

"Can't you tell them we'll pay them tomorrow? I'm hungry!" Hypatia flung herself into an armchair, and scowled.

Her mother clasped her hands together imploringly. "Hypatia – dearest girl! Your dear, devoted Papa has gone to his resting place among the stars, and we must learn to manage without him. Be patient! Be kind!"

Hypatia gave a very unladylike snort. "That's rubbish, Mother, and you know it. Father wasn't the least little bit devoted: he didn't even know my name half the time, and he only remembered yours when he was sober. All he cared about was having a good time."

Before her mother could answer, Affogato came marching in. "Mother! My riding boots haven't been cleaned! And nobody's answering the bell! And I looked out of the window, and what do you think I saw? Cook was—"

"Leaving." Hypatia glared at her brother. "I've just told her. And who cares about your boots? I want my lunch. I'm hungry!"

Arabella Poskett looked at her children in despair. Weak-chinned and opinionated, they were the spitting image of their father. Despite a succession of governesses and tutors, they had never shown any sign of having learned anything useful – and useful was what she desperately needed at the present moment.

"Oh!" A faint glimmer of hope made her brighten. "Hypatia, is Robert still here? He's *so* efficient..."

Hypatia shook her head. "He was one of the first to go. I never knew butlers had so much luggage – I mean, what does a butler want with five suitcases? He had all these bags with him as well, and they clinked and rattled and looked ever so hugely heavy."

A terrible suspicion crept into Arabella's mind and she leapt to her feet. Leaving her children staring after her, she hurried down the corridor to the butler's pantry ... where she found every drawer hanging open, and every silver spoon, knife and fork gone.

Running to the kitchen she found that was almost as bare; the dented iron saucepans were left, but the rows of shining copper pans had vanished.

"Oh nooooo..." she wailed, and hurried to the larder. That, too, was all but empty; only a mouldy meat pie and a couple of wilting carrots remained.

"It's all gone, Ma'am," said a small squeaky voice, and Arabella jumped.

"Who's that?"

"It's only me, Ma'am: Edie Boiler. I'm your kitchen maid, Ma'am."

Turning, Arabella saw a small girl in a dress that was far too big for her. A grubby apron was tied twice round her very small waist, and her face was smudged with dirt. She bobbed a curtsey, and coughed apologetically. "I did say as it was unfair to take it all, you being a poor lonely widow and all, but they wouldn't listen. They was very angry, Ma'am. Robert said as he was owed more than three months wages, Cook said the same – and so did all the rest." She shrugged her skinny shoulders. "I could make you a cup of tea, Ma'am, if you'd like one. I've got some tea leaves hidden in a tin in the boot room. And there's milk in the dairy: they couldn't take that, although they would've if they could."

"Thank you, Edie." Arabella looked more closely at the diminutive kitchen maid. Her face was dirty, but her eyes were bright, and she was smiling sympathetically. No one had offered the Honourable Henry Poskett's widow the slightest sympathy since his demise, and even a smile was something to be grateful for. "That's kind of you…" She paused. "But aren't you owed wages as well?"

Edie put her head on one side. "Wages, Ma'am? I don't get them. I get 'Board and Lodging' and 'Be Grateful'. I'm from the work-house, see, so I don't count for nothing."

Arabella stared at her in astonishment. "Goodness! I never knew we had a workhouse child here!"

"And now you'll want me to go." Edie sounded resigned. "Everyone always does when they finds out. That Lady Figgis – that's where I was last – she didn't even let me stay the night. But's that's life, as the ellythump said to the clown after he'd squashed him flat. Do you want me to make you a cuppa first, Ma'am? Or pack right now?"

"Oh no!" Arabella was thinking fast. "Please stay! I'm going to need all the help I can get, and you seem to be a practical girl…"

"I'm that all right." Edie nodded. "You just ask me, Ma'am. Anything I can do, I will." She straightened her apron, and beamed at her employer. "They used to call me the Cork at the workhouse, Ma'am – things got ever so bad sometimes, but I always bobbed up again."

She was interrupted by the door opening; Affogato and Hypatia came storming in. "So there you are, Mother!" Affogato put his hands on his hips. "We've been looking for you everywhere!"

"That's right!" Hypatia agreed. "And where's our lunch?" Her eye fell on Edie, and her lip curled. "*Yeuch!* What have we here? Something that's crawled out from under the sink? Be off with you, girl ... unless you can cook." She peered at the little kitchen maid. "Well? *Can* you?"

"Ain't much to cook with," Edie told her. "But if you don't mind waiting a moment, I can see if there's any eggs. They did try to take the chickens, but they couldn't catch them."

Hypatia immediately sat down at the kitchen table. "A cheese soufflé, perhaps? Or an *omelette à la Russe*. But do make sure it's soft in the middle."

"I can do scramble," Edie said cheerfully. "It's

that or nothing. Always supposing there are any eggs, that is. You can take a hen to the nest, but you can't make her lay." And she trotted out of the kitchen.

Affogato sat down beside his sister. "So when do we get another cook, Mother?" He yawned. "And do be sure she can make pastry. The old one had SUCH a heavy hand; her apple pies were appalling. Gave me indigestion every time."

Arabella Poskett took a deep breath. The thought that she had an ally – albeit a very small and grubby one – was making her brave. "There won't be another cook, Affie. You have to understand, we've got no money. Just debts. We're going to have to think of a way to keep ourselves alive – and it's not going to be easy. Not at all. We'll have to sell everything we can... We may even have to sell Uncaster Hall."

"WHAT?" Affogato went white and Hypatia green with shock and horror.

"Sell...? Sell ... Uncaster ... Hall?" Affogato could hardly get the words out. "But we can't! We absolutely can't! Where would we live? Where would I keep my horses?"

"There won't be any horses," their mother told them. "Well – maybe one, just so we can get around."

Her children were now looking like goldfish, their mouths wide open and their eyes bulging. "NO HORSES?"

"So you knows about the horses?" Edie had come back into the kitchen, clutching a basket of golden brown eggs. "Robert, he took them all – except the old one, Bertha. She weren't no use to him. Said he'd take the nags to the livery stables, 'cos they're owed too ... and they'd see he got his wages all proper from the sale."

She put the eggs on the table.

"So who's for scramble, then?"

Three

VINCENT VON GREAZLE, A MEMBER OF THE Pringle Players from the beginning, was 50 years old. Now grey, grizzled and missing his front teeth, he was no longer able to play the Noble Hero unless the lights were exceptionally dim. Worrying about his future made him tetchy. From time to time, after a particularly heated argument, Pa Pringle threatened to dismiss him; but everyone knew this was unlikely to happen. He was too much part of the family: Charlie and Rosie called him Uncle Vinnie, even though he was no relation, and they were fond of him – he told them stories, and often slipped a penny into their pockets.

Returning with his wife after a brief family visit, Vinnie was astonished to find the company not only had a new name, but had determined on a New Beginning. He was peevish at first, but his wife – known to audiences as "Miss Gertrude Gracegirdle, the Canary of Covent Garden", and to the Pringle family as "Gertie" – told him not to be silly.

"Really, Vinnie! Can't you recognize an opportunity when you see one? A whole new audience! And travel, as well. Sounds more than splendid to me. I'm bored to death with London and singing in back rooms for half-nothing. If you don't want to come you can stay right here, and I'll go on my own."

Vinnie, who was half his wife's size, knew when to give in. "I was only saying, dear heart—"

"Well, don't." Gertie glared at him, then turned to Ma Pringle. "So, what's going to happen to the horse? Going to sell her to the knacker's yard?"

Rosie had just come in with Charlie. They had been singing to entertain the queues outside the music hall, and Charlie's cap was full of farthings and halfpennies; but Rosie's cheerful expression vanished as she heard what Gertie was saying. "No! That's a horrible,

29

horrible idea! We can't ever sell darling Hetty!"

Gertie raised her eyebrows. "No good being sentimental, Rosie. The knacker's yard pays good money for horse-meat, and money's what's needed right now."

Aunt Mags folded her arms – she had been persuaded to take her flannel petticoats to the pawnbroker earlier in the day, and was feeling the cold. "It certainly is."

"You're cruel, both of you!" Rosie stamped her foot. "Hetty's one of the family! You wouldn't send me or Charlie or baby Joe to the knacker's yard, would you?"

Seeing a storm blowing up, Ma handed the baby to Charlie and put her arm round Rosie's shoulders. "Don't you worry, my pet. It's all sorted. I'm staying here with Sally-Ann and the little ones, and Mr Dobbs is going to keep Hetty and use her for his grocery deliveries. She's not too old to pull a little cart full of carrots and apples, and it'll help Mr Dobbs ever such a lot. What's more, it'll go towards paying what we owe."

Rosie gave a gasp. Her face pale and her lip trembling, she stared at her mother. "Ma, you

can't stay here! What'll we do without you? Pa –
tell her! She's got to come! She's *got* to!"

"Now, now!" Ma hugged Rosie tighter.
"You're a big girl, Rosie. You and Charlie, you're
part of the company. And think about it! We
don't know what it'll be like in the North, or
where you'll be staying. Could be snow and ice
and howling winds for all we know – and Little
Billy, he gets colds at the drop of a hat. No ... Pa
and I have talked it over, and it makes much
more sense for me to wait here with the little
ones. Think what a lot you'll have to tell me
when you get back!"

Rosie's stomach felt hollow – as if she hadn't
eaten for a fortnight. "It's the money, isn't it?"
she said. "There's no money for your ticket!"
She dug in her pocket, untwisted her hankie
and pulled out a silver three-penny bit. "See?
People even give us silver! We can all go, Ma ...
we really, really can!"

Ma gave Rosie one last squeeze before taking
the bawling baby back. As she began to rock him
to sleep, she said, "It's no good fussing, pet. Pa's
going to try the North for a couple of months,
and see how it goes. If it's looking like the big

success that I'm sure it will be, he'll find lodgings for all of us – and then me and Sally-Ann and the little ones will come and join you."

"But what if it isn't a success, Ma?" Rosie asked. "Can we can come home then?"

Charlie had had enough. "You're such a baby, Rosie. I say we leave you behind and take Sally-Ann instead."

Sally-Ann bounced to her feet. "Take me! Take me, Charlie! I can be a norphan! I can sing! I can sing lots 'n' LOTS of songs!"

"Really, Charlie!" Ma Pringle was not pleased. "I have enough trouble with Sally-Ann without you putting ideas into her head! Rosie's going, and that's that. Now, seeing as you've got that silver threepence, why don't you run down the road and fetch us some meat-pies?"

The thought of pies cheered everyone, and the evening ended peacefully enough – but after Rosie and Charlie had gone to bed, and Vinnie had taken the Covent Garden Canary home to their lodgings, Pa, Ma and Aunt Mags talked late into the night.

"Be kind to Rosie, Mags," Ma said. "Charlie's tough, but Rosie – she's up and down like the weather. And it's likely to be longer than a couple of months. That's right, isn't it Pa?"

"Could well be," Pa agreed. "No need to tell her, though."

Aunt Mags sniffed. "It's a hard life. She needs to get used to it." Softening a little, she added, "But I'll keep an eye on her."

Four

THINGS WERE GOING FROM BAD TO WORSE at Uncaster Hall. Affogato and Hypatia, having eaten a huge plateful of scrambled eggs, had retired to their adjoining bedrooms and locked themselves in. After a while, a note was pushed out from under the door of Affogato's room; Arabella, trudging upstairs to plead with her children, read it with some difficulty:

Mother! Altho you dont deserve the name of mother becos mothers are ment to LOOK AFTER there offspring! It is yor DUTY! Our nobble queen Victorria is an egsample you shood FOLLOW!

Wen you come to yor senses you can

tell us and we will come out. Untill then
we are ditermined to stay here and we
have swarn so to do in BLUD.

   Affogato and Hypatia Poskett

P.S. We have got the chikens so we can
eet eggs.

Edie had come up behind Arabella, and when
she was passed the note she read it in silence.

"Cor," she said as she finished. "They spells
worse than me! Didn't they go to school?"

Arabella shook her head. "They had tutors.
They were supposed to be the best, but I don't
think the dear children tried very hard."

"'Tooters'?" This was not a word Edie recognized. "I don't like the sound of them. But my
gran always said, 'It's not learning that matters:
it's living.' And, Ma'am – if you'll 'scuse me
asking – how are you going to live?" She went
pink. "'Scuse me again, but there was a lot of
talk in the kitchen, and I couldn't help but hear
it. We got folk banging on the door asking
about bills, see, and then there was the wages
not being paid ... Cook said as she reckoned the

bailiffs would be round any day, and that's why she took them copper pans." Her blush deepened. "Sorry, Ma'am."

Arabella Poskett was silent. She was the only child of a widower – James T. Merriweather, who had made his fortune in linens, cotton and sewing thread. Her father had been less than delighted when the Honourable Henry Poskett asked for her hand in marriage. Suspecting Henry was after his daughter's money, he had waited until the extremely expensive wedding was over before announcing he was not going to pay for anything else until the Honourable Henry found gainful employment.

This had never happened; Henry felt strongly that any form of mental or physical work was beneath him. Assuming his wealthy father-in-law would eventually pay his debts, he had spent wildly and enthusiastically ... but James T. Merriweather was a man of his word. Not a single debt was paid. He had visited his daughter when Affogato was born, but Henry had made it abundantly clear he was unwelcome so James T. Merriweather left after just two days swearing never to return.

As their debts mounted, Arabella sent pleading letters – but they were returned unopened and she had eventually stopped writing, taking to selling small items of jewellery in an attempt to make ends meet. Eventually the news reached her that James T. Merriweather's empire had collapsed and the owner gone missing: no further details were available, and Arabella had given up hope of ever seeing her father again.

Seeing her deep in thought, Edie coughed. "Got an idea, Ma'am, if you don't mind my mentioning it..."

Arabella stood up straight. There was no point in thinking about James T. Merriweather. "What is it, Edie?" she asked.

"Well..." Edie fidgeted with her apron strings. "It's like this, Ma'am. My friend Minnie's Auntie Lou, her little tobacco business went bust, see. Not a penny to her name – and bills! Lord love us, she had bills. But she had a spare room, and she began to let it out. Only single ladies, mind. No riff-raff! Then she moved into the kitchen so she had two rooms to let ... and before long she'd made enough to rent a bigger house where she could let four or five rooms, and now she's living in luxury."

A wistful look came over Edie's thin little face.

"Guess what, Ma'am! She has roast chicken every week! A fat one, too ... none of your scraggy old birds. *AND* she's got a real Nottingham lace shawl! My friend Minnie says it's a wonder. It's about growing an oak from a little haycorn, see. That's what you need: a little haycorn."

Arabella had got lost in the complications of Edie's story. "You mean I should grow trees?"

"Trees?" Edie burst into peals of laughter. "No! I meant as you could take in lodgers, Ma'am! This big old place ... there's loads and loads of room!"

"Lodgers? Oh – oh dear." Arabella sounded doubtful. "I'm not sure. I'm not sure at all..."

Edie looked wise. "Tell you what. Start with theatricals: actors, that is. They don't stay long. Always up and off and away, so you could see how things go – and they won't expect luxury, Ma'am."

"Actors?" Arabella was imagining large, be-whiskered gentlemen, booming complaints as they paced to and fro wearing out the carpets, and well-endowed women, being dramatic about the absence of marmalade. "But are they respectable? I have my children to consider, remember. Darling Affogato is so easily led astray."

"They're as respectable as most, Ma'am." Edie bobbed a curtsey. "Another cup of tea? Things always look better after a cuppa."

Arabella Poskett was exhausted. Her life had turned upside down, and everything that had made it pleasurable was draining away at a terrifying speed. Only the little kitchen maid, still smiling cheerfully, stood between her and total despair. "Thank you," she said. "That would be lovely."

"We'd better make it four cups, Ma'am." Edie was on tiptoe, peering out of the landing window. "If I ain't much mistaken, that's the bailiffs riding up. Recognize a bailiff anywhere, I would – I seen enough of them to last a lifetime. And they've got a empty cart coming up behind them, so they looks as if they mean business."

"Bailiffs?" Her employer sank down on the

stairs and clutched her head. Total despair came rushing round the corner, and leapt upon her. "BAILIFFS? Oh, the shame of it! The disgrace! Oh, Edie – whatever shall I do? This is the end ... the end of everything."

Edie put her hands on her hips. "Nothing ain't over until you're four foot underground with a big stone angel standing on your toes. We'll give them a cup of tea and talk nice, and see what we can do." She gave Arabella a hopeful glance. "Thought any more about letting those rooms, Ma'am? If we can say we got a plan to bring in the pennies they might go easier on you."

"Whatever you say, Edie."

And the owner of Uncaster Hall followed her kitchen maid obediently down the stairs, like a large paddle-steamer being towed by a very small tugboat.

Five

IT WAS A DULL, FOGGY MORNING WHEN THE Steam Whistle Theatre Company took their third-class seats in the ten-past-ten North Western train, each with a ticket for Uncaster. Pa would have liked to have made York their destination, but this proved to be too expensive; still, Uncaster was three hours north of London, and the more he thought about it the more sensible it seemed to begin in a small market town where there would be little to no competition. By the time the day of travel arrived, he had persuaded himself that he had made a remarkably intelligent decision.

Much to his regret, the company was not as thrilled to be starting out on their New Beginning as he was. Aunt Mags clutched a wicker

basket stuffed with her most precious possessions and stared grimly at the floor. Vinnie
was sulking because a couple of ragamuffin
lads had asked him if he'd left his teeth on the
mantelpiece, and the Canary of Covent Garden
was just as sulky because a porter had told her
to "Move along there, old lady!" Rosie was
red-eyed and tearful after a failed last minute
attempt to persuade Ma to come with them.
Ma, trying hard not to cry herself, was standing on the platform holding baby Joe. Little
Billy, Betty and Sally-Ann were close beside
her, Sally-Ann clutching her old rag doll.

Only Charlie was whistling happily; Pa looked
at him approvingly. "Run and check they've put
all the hampers in the luggage van," he said.
"Should be three of them. Make sure the costumes are on top. Don't want them crushed!"

"On my way, Pa," Charlie said, and he
jumped down onto the platform and ran to the
end of the train.

The luggage van was full of every shape and
every kind of box, bag and case. Climbing inside,
Charlie was surprised to see a curious-looking
black box tucked in next to the Steam Whistle

Theatre Company's wicker baskets. Intrigued, he bent over the faded luggage-label and read: "Little Baby Bubbles, the One and Only Child Master of Magic and Escapology."

"Oi-oi! Peeking and prying?" A porter had arrived to close the van doors. "Luggage only in 'ere. Scarper!"

Jumping down, Charlie hurried to find his family. Seeing Ma, he took the opportunity to give her a last hug and to blow kisses to the little ones.

"Be a good boy, Charlie," Ma said. "And—" with an effort she swallowed the lump in her throat— "have fun. We'll see you soon."

"Bye, Ma," Charlie said, and hugged her again. This was too much for Ma; she began to cry, at the same time pushing him away.

"Get on the train, dearest boy," she said. "I'm sorry. I can't bear to watch you go." She turned away, half-blinded by the tears running down her cheeks, and disappeared into the crowded station. Betty, sobbing, walked beside her, and Little Billy wailed loudly in sympathy as he was hauled along by Sally-Ann.

Charlie took a deep breath. He was not a

hard-hearted boy, but the thought of the adventure ahead easily overcame his sorrow at having to say goodbye to his mother. *Poor Ma*, he said to himself. *But she can come and join us soon, and then we'll all be together again.*

After opening the heavy carriage door with some difficulty, he found two strangers had taken the last seats. One was an elderly woman, knitting a long grey sock, and the other was her bespectacled companion, who was reading a book. Neither looked particularly happy to be sharing the carriage with the Steam Whistle Theatre Company.

Pa, ever the entertainer, was doing his best to cheer everyone along. "Bear up, Mags! And give us a smile, Vinnie. Bet they've never seen a Noble Hero where we're going. Or heard anyone sing like you do, Gertie. Rosie! Wipe your eyes! It's a New Beginning, remember. By this time next year we'll be rich and famous, and we'll have Ma and the little ones eating meat-pies every night. Just you wait and see!"

Rosie looked at him mournfully. "You said we'd be rich and famous when we were booked to play at old Mother Milligan's Supper Rooms,

Pa, and we weren't. And you said it again when it was that horrible smelly top room at The Blue Boar, but we got booed off the stage. And you said it again when it was—"

Pa silenced her with a wave of his hand. "When the right audiences come, we'll be rich and famous. That's all we need: the right audiences."

Charlie began to laugh, but stopped when Aunt Mags glared at him.

"It's not funny. We do a good show, we do. All that holds us back is a lack of appreciation amongst the people we play to." She snorted. "I'll be interested to see if they're any better when we reach the foreign places. Probably never even heard of old Bill Shakespeare up there in – what's that place we're going to? 'Uncaster'. It'll be hard work, you mark my words."

Pa Pringle was spared from replying by a long and piercing whistle. A moment later, the train began to move. Aunt Mags screamed and clutched her basket more closely to her chest, while Charlie looked eagerly out of the windows. Rosie, rubbing her eyes, came to sit beside him. At first, thick clouds of steam meant that they couldn't see anything, but the world outside the carriage windows started to reappear as the train pulled away from the station and settled into a steady *CHUFF-chuff-chuff-chuff* ... and they both gasped as they saw the speed at which they were travelling.

"It's like flying!" Rosie said, her tears forgotten. "Look, there's a tumbledown old house – and now we're beside it – and now it's gone! I've never been as fast as this!"

"Beats a horse and cart," Charlie agreed. "Bet we're faster than even the fastest stagecoach!"

Aunt Mags moaned faintly. "If any of us live to tell the tale, which I very much doubt, I want little Sally-Ann to have my best white kid gloves to remember me by."

"Nonsense, Mags! You'll be wearing those for years yet!" Pa rubbed his hands together. "Have a look out of the window."

"I'm not looking out until we've stopped. And it's no use trying to persuade me." Aunt Mags leant back in her seat and shut her eyes.

Charlie grinned at Rosie. "Doesn't know what she's missing," he said. "Look! We're nearly out of London already! Hey, Rosie – we're heading north ... watch out for bears!"

"Bears?" Rosie looked anxious, but Pa laughed and patted her knee.

"He's teasing, Rosie pet. You're quite safe. Now, how about we learn something new? I've been thinking we need to freshen up our repertoire, seeing as we're on the path to fame and fortune. Shakespeare ... that's the chap for us. So I'm working on a new version of *King Lear*, where he and Cordelia recite a poem that'll bring a tear to every eye." Pa beamed happily at his family. "*'Oh daughter dear, You must not fear, For we will rule together. I say to you, I love you true, So never mind the weather.'* One of my best, if I do say so myself. That'll be me as Lear, of course, and you as Cordelia, Rosie. And I thought we could cheer it up with a song or two as well."

Pa pulled a sheet of music out of his pocket.

"And I've got something special for you, Gertie. A Marie Lloyd song!"

The bespectacled companion put her book down. "This, my dear Sir, is a public railway carriage – not a common music hall. Kindly desist from singing, or doing anything of the sort! My dear—" she tapped the elderly lady on the knee— "I'm sure you agree with me."

The elderly lady leant forward, her hand to her ear. "Eh? What was that? 'Cup of tea', did you say?"

Rosie began to giggle and the bespectacled companion glared at her, before tut-tutting angrily and burying herself once more in her book.

Pa, not in the least bothered by the objection, handed the song sheet to the Canary of Covent Garden. "There you go. It's a song about Life being Magic. I got it off the doorman at the Empire Theatre – it's the best thing going in London!"

Gertie forgot her irritation. She had always been envious of the great Marie Lloyd: she had never been able to understand why she, Miss Gertrude Gracegirdle, was not as famous. She considered herself just as attractive as Miss Lloyd (her nose might be bigger, but that was a sign of Character); she hardly ever sang flat; and if she occasionally forgot her words – well! That meant nothing.

She took the paper, and began murmuring happily to herself.

Six

AT THE OTHER END OF THE TRAIN, ANOTHER passenger was far from happy. Little Baby Bubbles was officially aged eight, but possessed an astonishing knowledge of events that had happened before his stated date of birth. Today he was cross, and making quite certain his dear Mama knew all about it.

"I'm not comfortable, I'm not comfortable at all. Why can't we go in First Class, with all the smart ladies and gentlemen? I'm a star, aren't I? I'm Little Baby Bubbles, Magician, and this is *horrid*. There aren't any cushions and I'm being bumped and rattled – and I don't like it!"

"Hush, Baby dear. It's not for much longer ... we'll be there in a few hours." Eliza Snicket dug in her large bag. "Here, have a lovely pork pie, darling. It's your favourite!"

"I *HATE* pork pies," Baby scowled. "And what do you mean, a few hours? You said it was only a short journey!"

"Oh, but it is! That nice young man at the station said we'd be there soon after lunchtime. So much quicker than the stagecoach! Why, I remember when I first came to London from Uncaster it took me two days: I had to spend the night in a shockingly damp inn, and I caught the most dreadful cold—"

"Who cares about you?" Baby flung himself back in his seat. "And who cares about Uncaster? You're always going on about it and it's boring. It sounds like a beastly place and I never ever want to go there."

His mother hesitated before answering. "Dearest one ... you know I said we were going to York? And we'd be performing at Mrs Moore's Supper Rooms? Well, Mrs Moore's Supper Rooms aren't ... aren't *exactly* in York."

A suspicious glint awoke in Baby's sharp little eyes. "What do you mean? Have you been telling me fibs?" A terrible idea made him sit bolt upright. "Don't you dare tell me we're going to Uncaster!"

Mrs Snicket shrugged. "I had to lie just a very little bit, my darling – but yes. That's where we're going. If I'd told you before, you'd never have got on the train." Her voice rose. "I couldn't afford tickets to York! I've tried to keep it from you, dearest, but we're nearly penniless. We need a new start, and Uncaster will be just the right place. So be my dear, kind, darling boysie, and let's make the best of it together."

Baby had been staring at his mother, his face growing darker and darker. As she finished her plea, he let out an ear-piercing scream. "Stop the train! Stop the train RIGHT NOW THIS MINUTE, or I'll ... I'll throw myself out of the window!"

A sailor in the corner seat – who had been unashamedly listening to everything that had been said – looked at him with interest. "Give you a hand if you like, young fellow-me-lad. Always happy to help."

Mrs Snicket turned on him. "'Young fellow', Mr Captain? He's just a little boy! Can't you see?

He's just a dear little boy who's terribly, terribly unhappy!"

The sailor grunted, and pulled his pipe from his pocket. "Doesn't look much like a little boy to me. I'd give him fourteen, at the least. He's about to burst the buttons off that there velvet suit of his, and that's the truth of it."

Baby glowered, but the sailor was busy filling his pipe and took no notice. Spoiling for a fight, Baby pounced on his mother instead. "You've gone mad! That's what it is ... you've gone mad! I'll get you certified and sent to Bedlam, that's what I'll do! I'll get you put away in a cell for ever and ever and ever, and I'll make sure they NEVER let you out!"

The sailor, his pipe now lit to his satisfaction, puffed a cloud of evil-smelling smoke and remarked, "If anyone were to ask me – which they won't – I'd say any 'little boy' as thinks as he can get his poor old Ma locked up deserves a right good spanking."

This was too much: Baby flew into a hysterical tantrum and began to stamp his feet and scream as loudly as he could. Mrs Snicket, with one eye on the sailor, wrung her hands in helpless agony – but the sailor puffed peacefully on his pipe.

"Slap him," he advised. "Had an aunt who used to throw wobblers. Only way to stop it."

The train gave such a sudden lurch that Baby was thrown across the compartment onto the seat opposite, sending the contents of his mother's carpet bag scattering in all directions. He landed with a yell and collapsed into a heap, sobbing as loudly as he could manage.

"Oh, my poor, poor darling!" Mrs Snicket patted Baby's shoulder with one hand, while searching through her possessions with the other. She was looking for her smelling salts, but by the time she found them Baby's sobs had faded away and been replaced by gentle snoring.

The sailor grunted his approval. "Best thing after a wobbler. My aunt was a terror for them, but after forty winks she'd be right as rain. Where are you off to, Ma'am?"

"Uncaster," Mrs Snicket said as she settled herself next to the sailor. She gave him a sideways look. "Might you be going there yourself?"

The sailor shook his head. "No, no. Next station, me." He patted his pocket. "Got a sovereign or two to spend. I've been away on the high seas, but now I'm home for good. I've a mind to treat my dear old mother, and buy her a few comforts now she's old and ailing."

"Oh dear." Eliza Snicket gave him what she believed to be a winning smile. "I was hoping for a fine strong man to help me with my luggage. We're all alone in the world, me and my lovely boy." She heaved a sigh. "I wasn't born into the travelling life. A tragedy changed everything, and here I am: all alone."

She sighed again, and waited for the sailor to ask for more – but he sat silently smoking.

"Yes, all alone." She patted her hair. "But I had a great uncle in Uncaster, and I know it well; I often stayed there as a child. Things have been a little difficult lately, you see..."

"Trouble with the lad?" the sailor asked.

"Oh goodness no!" Mrs Snicket shook her head. "It's not my darling Baby's fault. He's a VERY talented magician and escapologist, just like his father – but we've had a few little problems with engagements. The theatres and music halls don't want us any more. It's SUCH a mystery!"

She paused, remembering the pile of letters cancelling Baby's bookings. There had been accusations of theft from a couple of well-known theatres, accusations so ridiculous that Mrs Snicket had torn up the letters and thrown away the pieces... But rumours had flown from venue to venue, with disastrous consequences.

"He used to be all the rage in North London," she went on. "A dear sweet little boy who could do the most amazing magic tricks – he was SO wonderful! He'd get encore after encore, until the poor darling was quite worn out. And you should have heard them roar when he escaped from a tank of jellyfish. But it's not like that now. We've had hardly any money coming in, so we've had to leave our lodgings."

She did not think it necessary to explain that they had left in the middle of the night, taking the landlady's silver teaspoons with them.

"But I'm sure once we get to Uncaster it'll all be wonderful again. I wrote to Mrs Moore, who runs the Supper Rooms, and she said she'd book Baby for three weeks – longer, if he's a success, and of course he will be. I know the clientele will be VERY superior, so we won't have any of the troubles we had in London."

Puffing steadily on his pipe, the sailor listened in silence. As Mrs Snicket finished, he grunted, and waved a wisp of smoke away. "All the rage, was he? Don't hold with magic tricks, myself." He gave the sleeping Baby a thoughtful look. "What's his real name, then?"

It took Baby's mother a moment to remember. She had called him "Baby" since he was born; it had been his father who had formally named him, two days before he disappeared on the arm of a much-bespangled bareback rider.

"Horace," she said at last. "That's it: Horace Snicket. Horace after his father, 'Slippery Horace Snicket, Magical Maestro'." She gave the sailor a coy glance from under her eyelashes. "I expect you'll know the name? He played all the big theatres. Once he even sawed the Prince of Wales in half!"

"Never heard of him." The sailor saw the surprise in Mrs Snicket's face, and added, "But that doesn't mean he wasn't famous. Like I said, I don't hold with magic." He tapped his pipe out on the floor of the compartment and stood up. "Next stop's mine. Take a tip from an old man who's seen downs as well as ups in this world of ours: you're a mother, and mothers don't always see too well when it comes to their sons. Get a dazzle in their eye, they do, and see swans where everyone else sees ducks – and the ducks start thinking that swans is what they are, and *that* leads to trouble."

He stuffed the pipe in his pocket, slung his bag on his back and – as the train pulled into the station – raised a hand in farewell.

Eliza Snicket waved a merry handkerchief until he was out of sight, then sank back in her seat. "What a despicably vulgar man. How dare he speak to me like that?" Baby stirred and grunted in his sleep, and her face softened. "But I have my darling boy – and together, we'll conquer the world..."

Seven

THE TWO MEN RIDING UP TO UNCASTER Hall were indeed bailiffs. Edie led them into the kitchen; tea was offered but rejected, and a long list of claims was produced – with terrifying threats of a debtors' prison if pounds, shillings and pence were not immediately forthcoming. It was Edie who suggested brandy and water; the atmosphere lightened at once and she hurried off to the wine cellar ... but came back looking despondent.

"Been cleared out," she reported. "Not a bottle left. All I got is a jug of Cook's home-made elderflower cordial."

An hour later, it was apparent that the elderflower cordial packed an unexpected punch. Both bailiffs were sitting at the kitchen table with their feet up, the debtors' prison forgotten. Instead, there was now cheery talk of a stay of execution, and an agreement that the removal of the furniture and pictures from the drawing room would be more than sufficient for the time being. Edie explained that money would soon be rolling in, and that it was essential to keep enough furniture to provide the expected lodgers with a degree of comfort.

The older bailiff nodded sagely, while trying to suppress a hiccup. "Too true," he said. "Too true. Lotsh and *lotsh* of lodgers ... eashily pay the billsh." He waved a hand vaguely in the direction of Arabella, who was nervously walking up and down. "Lotsh and lotsh of billsh ... poor, poor lady. But I has the *hoff* ... the *soff* ... the *shofftest* of hearts." He placed a large hand on his soiled waistcoat. "Trush ... trusht in me, dear lady."

The younger bailiff, after a regretful look at the now empty jug, heaved himself to his feet.

"Must be off," he said. "But my friend is right. Right as rain. Rain in Spain." He giggled, and winked at Edie who pretended not to notice. "Must be off. Job to do. Job-bob-bobbitty-boo!"

It took the combined efforts of the younger bailiff, Edie and Arabella to get the older bailiff out into the fresh air. Partially restored, he managed to climb on his horse and the two men rode away, swaying but upright. The three burly carters, who had been given the vaguest of instructions, advanced on the drawing room; Edie and an anxious Arabella accompanied them.

Having seen their employers riding away in an elderflower-cordial-induced haze, the men were not disposed to be particularly thorough. They were happy to remove the many large and exuberant pictures of hunting scenes that Arabella had always disliked, and to pile the cart with brisk little sofas and occasional tables that nobody had ever found occasion to use. A selection of silver-plated candelabras, decorated with unattractively bulbous cherubs, completed the load – and they drove away, leaving the room considerably emptier.

"Never did like those slobbery hunting dogs," Edie said cheerfully, as they made their way back to the kitchen. "Used to give me the creeps when I was clearing out the grate."

Arabella sank down on a chair. "Edie – what dreadful men those bailiffs were! Whatever would I have done without you?"

"It's Cook we should be thanking." Edie picked up the jug, and sniffed it. "Cor blimey! Doesn't half smell strong! No wonder they was half-seas-over." Seeing Arabella's blank look, she added, "I means 'drunk', Ma'am."

"Oh." Arabella sighed. "Yes ... I did recognize the symptoms."

"I'm sure you did, Ma'am," Edie said. "Now, I don't want to push you, Ma'am, but what's done today is better than what's left for tomorrow. Should we look at the rooms? The rooms for letting? And Ma'am – you've got ever such classy handwriting. Why don't you write out a few cards? Saying: 'Rooms to Let at Uncaster Hall. Short lets only. Terms on application.'"

Arabella blinked. "Terms?"

Edie smiled. "You know, Ma'am: the rent. Mustn't put it in writing on the card, see. What you does is size 'em up, and then you do a bit of argy-bargying. Makes them feel they got a bargain, when all the time it's what you was wanting."

Arabella Poskett was beginning to wonder if she was fast asleep, and dreaming the most extraordinary dream. She was in a world she knew nothing about, and her only guide was a small girl with smuts on her nose and a beaming smile.

She rubbed a weary hand over her eyes, and stood up. "We'll do exactly as you say, Edie," she said. "But first … is there another apron? We'll save the tea as a treat for later."

Eight

B Y THE TIME THE TRAIN REACHED UNCASTER, Charlie and Rosie had decided that this was the only way to travel. Even Aunt Mags had opened her eyes for the last few miles, although she refused to acknowledge there was anything positive about the speed with which they had reached their destination.

"It's not right," she said. "Just you wait and see. You'll find you've left more than half your brain behind, and it'll take at least three days for it to catch up. If God had meant us to go this fast, he'd have given us an extra pair of legs."

"Come along, come along!" Pa stood up, gathering as many bags and cases and parcels as he could carry. "We've got to get the hampers, remember!" His large round face was shining with excitement, and he opened the compartment door with a flourish. "Ladies and gentlemen of the Steam Whistle Theatre Company – welcome to Fame and Fortune!"

Rosie and Charlie hurried after him. Once they were on the platform, Pa hustled them towards the luggage van. Two porters were heaving the wicker hampers out; the strange black box that Charlie had noticed earlier was already propped against a pillar.

"That yours?" a porter asked. Pa shook his head, and the porter looked at the label. "'Little Baby Bubbles, the One and Only Child Master of Magic and Escapology'. Escapology? What's that when it's at home? Never heard of one of them before." He turned the label over, and shouted at a large man leaning on the wall outside the ticket office. "Oi! Delivery for you! Got to go to the Supper Rooms!"

Rosie pulled at Pa's arm. "Did you hear, Pa? A baby who does magic! And what's 'escap' ... 'escap' ... the other thing?"

"You should know that, Rosie." Charlie said in lofty tones. "It means escaping from boxes, or tanks, or being tied up."

"Really?" Rosie was even more impressed. "Darling Pa, do say we can go and see him!"

"Maybe." Pa watched the large man swing the black box onto his shoulders and stride off towards the small donkey cart tied to a railing. "It'll be competition, pet. Still ... it's only a baby. What can he do?" Pa's natural optimism asserted itself. "And we've got Shakespeare! Bound to bring the audiences rolling in."

"That's for sure." Charlie nodded. "Where are we going now, Pa? Hey! We're not playing at the Supper Rooms too, are we?"

"No." Pa was counting coins from his pocket. "We're off to The Golden Lion. Ma heard about it from a lady who'd stayed there on her way down from York. There's a yard there, a yard with a nice little stage ... suit us down to the ground!" He turned to one of the porters. "How much for a carrier? Those hampers over there – property of the Steam Whistle Theatre Company, to go to The Golden Lion."

The porter shrugged. "Bert is the carrier here. And he's gone."

Pa's face fell, but a glance at the baskets made him brighten again. Each wicker basket had the name of the company emblazoned on the side in gold and scarlet, and he suddenly saw the opportunity for a little free publicity.

"We'll take them there ourselves," he announced – and then, wondering if he'd been rash, asked, "Is it far?"

"Golden Lion? Only a step away. Down t'high street, then first on right." The porter looked at Pa curiously. "Do them plays, do you?"

"Indeed we do!" Pa put his hands on his hips, and puffed out his chest. "Glorious Shakespeare! Comedy, history and tragedy; alarms, excursions and monologues; scenes of pathos to make you weep; scenes of terror to make you pale ... we have it all. Tell you what, my man – come along after we've settled in, and I'll let you in for free!"

"I'll think on it," was all the porter said, and he went off whistling.

Pa, somewhat deflated, called to his company. A few minutes later a strange procession left the station: Pa and a puffing Aunt Mags carrying the first hamper, Gertie and Charlie staggering under the weight of the second, and Vinnie and Rosie half-carrying, half-dragging the third.

"Once more unto the breach, my friends, my company, my children!" Pa declaimed as they made their way onto Uncaster high street. "On, on, my souls! Onward to glory, to victory, to fame!"

The Golden Lion was just off the main street: "nice and central", as Aunt Mags said. Nevertheless, the street was on a hill and the hampers were heavy. The company was hot and sweaty within minutes of setting out. Various passers-by stopped to stare as they struggled on their way; a large whiskery man driving a coal cart enraged the Canary of Covent Garden by asking if she was, "One of them high-kicking girls?" Several elderly matrons tut-tutted and shook their heads as the cavalcade went by. By the time they reached the door of The Golden Lion they were exhausted, and Charlie and Rosie's arms were aching badly.

Pa stopped outside to mop his brow and recover his dignity. "I shall go ahead and announce our arrival," he said. "And then we will gather together to discuss what to do next." His perspiring red face became hopeful. "It's quite possible that word has already reached our worthy landlord. We may even be applauded on entering this noble tavern!"

Pa's hopes were quickly dashed. The landlord, an enormous man with thick bushy eyebrows, was polishing pewter mugs at the bar and didn't even look up as Pa approached.

Pa cleared his throat. "My good man, I am delighted to inform you that the Steam Whistle Theatre Company is here at last!"

"What's that?" The landlord put down his cloth and peered suspiciously at Pa. "I bain't nobody's good man, and that's a fact. And who might you be, marching in here like the Lord of Rumplepooza?"

"My name is Frederick Pringle." Pa gave a small bow. "My esteemed wife wrote to inform you that the Steam Whistle Theatre Company would shortly be available to perform tragedy, comedy, and a variety of other dramatic works at The Golden Lion ... and lo! here we are!" He stepped back, expecting the landlord's suspicious scowl to melt into a welcoming smile.

Instead, the scowl grew darker. "Never had no letter like that." The landlord shook his head. "Anyways, we're booked for theatricals. So you'd best be off where you come from."

"Fred?" Aunt Mags appeared in the doorway. "Is there a problem? Oh! Excuse me, Sir. May I have the pleasure of introducing myself? Miss Margaretta Pringle. We are SO delighted to be here in your most excellent hostelry. Perhaps you might care to choose the first play from our extensive repertoire? Might I recommend *The Crowning of the Queen of Sheba?*"

"Sukie!" The landlord turned, and roared down the passage behind the bar. "SUKIE! There's a pair of dafties here, and one of 'em thinks she's the Queen of Sheba! Come and see before I throw them out."

A small, red-haired woman came bustling up the passage. When she saw Pa and Aunt Mags, she stopped. "Well I never," she said. "Londoners, or I'm a scratchrabbit! Whatever are you doing here, my dears? Lost your way?"

Aunt Mags had been taking in the furniture and fittings of The Golden Lion. *Rather too many broken windows for my liking*, she said to herself. *Still, the floors are clean enough.* She switched her attention to Sukie: "Yes, indeed! We hail from

69

London, but I'm sure my sister-in-law's letter explained how much we hope to be welcomed here in the North."

"Sukie, tell Lord Rumplepooza here we ain't had no letter." The landlord folded his arms. "And then I'll show them the door."

"Letter?" Sukie looked suddenly thoughtful. "But there was a letter, George." She screwed up her face as she tried to remember. "But it weren't about a lord. Or a Queen of Sheba – t'was about the little stage in our yard. What was the name now? Bungle? Pinkerton? No ... t'wasn't that..."

Charlie, who had crept in behind Aunt Mags, came hurrying forward. "I know!" he said. "It's not Pinkerton – it's Pringle! The Pringle Players! Ma wrote in such a hurry she must have forgotten we'd changed the name."

Sukie nodded. "That'll be the right of it. The Pringle Players. Coming here, they are. So we don't have no room for the likes of you, m'dear."

Relief made Aunt Mags sink down on the nearest chair. "But that's us! *We* are the Pringle Players! I am Miss Margaretta Pringle, and my brother here is Frederick Pringle, but we have a new name for the company, you see—"

Pa interrupted her. "That's right. We are now the Steam Whistle Theatre Company, Intrepid Travellers from South to North."

"Ho, yes?" The landlord, George, was unconvinced. "Seems mighty odd to me, changing names at a moment's notice. And what's wrong with 'Pringle'? The old Uncaster blacksmith, he were a Pringle. Right good man he were too, afore he died."

"That's why George said he'd let them use the yard," Sukie put in. "Said as it was a name he could trust." She shook her head. "We never had theatricals before, see, but we thought we'd try, just this once – seeing as it was a good respectable name. There's a lot in a name, George says."

"How right you are, madam. Our noble bard has much to say on the subject. Why, I could quote—" Pa was silenced by a sharp kick on the ankle.

"My dear brother knows the works of Mr Shakespeare all too well," Aunt Mags remarked, with a warning glare at Pa. "Now, might we see the stage? And do you have accommodation?" She saw Sukie's blank face. "I mean, do you have rooms for us? We're a company of six, but two are children."

It took another half an hour to persuade the suspicious George that the company was truly risen from the ashes of the Pringle Players. Even when Charlie showed him props and costumes labelled with the old name he remained doubtful, and flatly refused to allow Sukie to offer Pa rooms.

"I'll give them a month in the yard," he said. "Fair's fair. But I'll not have them staying in the house." He picked up his polishing cloth. "If they'd been what that letter said they was, I'd have thought on it. But all this chopping and changing – why, I don't hold with it and that's a fact. 'Steamy Whistlers'? What kind of a name is that? Show them the stage, Sukie. And make sure they don't make off with the candles!"

Seeing Pa turning a deep shade of crimson at this outrageous suggestion, Aunt Mags took his arm in a firm grip. "Come along, Fred. Charlie, run and call the others. They'll be wondering what's going on."

Charlie did as he was told, and found Gertie and Vinnie sitting on the wicker hampers. There was no sign of Rosie.

"Where's she gone?" he asked.

"Went to explore," Gertie told him. "She'll be back in a minute. What's it like?"

"Tricky," Charlie said. "And what's more, we've got nowhere to sleep tonight."

Nine

Little Baby Bubbles and his mother had a very different reception at Mrs Moore's Supper Rooms. Mrs Moore herself was waiting at the door, and there was a small crowd hovering hopefully in the street outside. As the cart rattled up there was a smattering of applause, and Baby stood up and bowed.

The children ignored him and the adults looked puzzled.

"*Eeeeh* ... that there's a well-fed lad," said a loud voice. "Likes his pies, and no mistake!"

A furious Baby sat down again, purple-faced and muttering. Mrs Snicket gave the onlookers a gracious wave, and hurried her son inside.

"I want to see the magic baby!" A small girl

tugged at her mother's arm. "Where's the baby, Mam?"

"*Sh*, pet. It must be in that big black box. Keep it safe, like." Her mother was watching Bert unloading the luggage. He didn't seem to be taking any special care: any baby unfortunate enough to be inside would be shaken black and blue. "We'll come and see the show tomorrow, lovey. You'll see him then, for sure."

Inside the Supper Rooms, Mrs Moore was just as puzzled. "If you don't mind my asking, is the child magician coming later?" she asked, as she put out the teacups. "On the next train, perhaps?"

Mrs Snicket's eyes opened very wide. "Oh no! This is Baby ... my darling little boy."

Mrs Moore looked at the darling little boy. He was almost as tall as she was, and easily twice as wide.

"This itches," he complained as he tugged irritably at his lace collar. "I want to take it off. And who were those stupid people outside? I didn't like them!"

"Goodness me..."

Mrs Moore had sold a number of tickets for the following night's performance, and had been counting on a comfortable income for another two weeks and possibly longer. Entertainment at the Supper Rooms usually consisted of elderly sopranos singing about little white lambs falling prey to the big bad wolf, or alternatively three hulking lads performing a clog dance whilst roaring a chorus of *Hey Diddle Diddle* and *Ho! for the Purple Hedgehog*. A professional child magician who was also an escapologist had caught the imagination of the local population, and there had been a steady queue clutching their shillings and sixpences ever since she put up the first poster.

"Does he shrink?" she asked hopefully.

"Shrink?" Baby's mother was baffled.

"Get smaller," Mrs Moore explained. "When he does his magic. And escaping. He does look quite big at the moment."

Mrs Snicket opened her mouth to protest, but at that moment Baby managed to disentangle himself from the offending collar. "Stupid thing," he said as he threw it on the floor. "I won't wear it again. Do you hear, Mother? I won't! It makes me look like a pig's head on a dish."

His mother sighed and picked up the

discarded collar. "It makes you look charming, Baby darling." She shook her head and smiled at Mrs Moore. "Boys! Do you have children, dear Mrs Moore?"

Mrs Moore was studying Baby, and didn't answer. He had flung himself into her favourite chair and was jingling a couple of coins in his pocket. Without thinking about what he was doing, he pulled one out and began flipping it in and out of his fingers so that it appeared to vanish, reappear, then vanish again.

Impressed, Mrs Moore decided that perhaps he wasn't quite as large as he had first appeared. After all, she had never met an underage magician before ... perhaps it was normal for them to be bigger than the average child.

"Your room is ready for you," she said. "I hope you'll be comfortable. I'm looking forward to your first performance, there's a good crowd booked in."

"That's wonderful news." Mrs Snicket hoped her smile didn't reveal how relieved she was.

"Let's hope he continues to be as sought after." Mrs Moore had read the smile with some accuracy. "You'll have competition after tomorrow. Most unusual, I have to say: there's some kind of theatre company coming to The Golden Lion ... and they're from London as well, I believe."

This was the last thing Mrs Snicket wanted to hear, but she kept her smile. "From London?" She gave a careless laugh to conceal her anxiety. "South London, I expect."

"I really don't know," Mrs Moore said. "I don't have much to do with the Lion. It's a very different type of establishment."

"Well, I'm sure darling Baby will outshine any horrid little touring company, wherever they come from." Mrs Snicket looked round, hoping to change the subject. "Such a lovely parlour! What exquisite taste you have, Mrs Moore. I'm so glad we were able to fit in an engagement here in your delightful rooms." She looked at Baby. "Did you hear, Baby darling? Clever Mrs Moore already has a lovely large audience for you!"

Baby shrugged, and tucked his feet up under him. "Make sure they don't want an encore. I don't like doing them. And I'm hungry! I want something to eat ... and I want it right now!"

"I'm afraid I don't serve supper until eight o'clock," Mrs Moore said. She looked again at the world famous child magician and escapologist. Despite his girth he had folded himself into a remarkably small space, and her hopes rose higher. "But I might, perhaps, be able to find a portion of steak and kidney pudding?"

"I suppose that'll do." Baby was ungracious but his mother fluttered round Mrs Moore praising her and thanking her, and the landlady called for one of the kitchen boys.

"Jago! Fetch our visitor a plate of the steak pudding, if you please. And be quick about it!"

"Oh, that would be so wonderfully kind!" Mrs Snicket clapped her hands in delight. "Baby will be so very, very grateful!"

A skinny youth with the small pink eyes of a weasel, Jago did as he was told. Baby, showing no signs of gratitude, consumed the entire plateful without pausing for breath. "More!" he demanded, and Jago was sent to the kitchen again.

As Baby wolfed down his second helping, Mrs Moore secretly resolved to put her rates up. Anyone who could eat as much as this lodger was going to have to pay extra, regardless of his talent or skill. *It's a good thing we haven't discussed terms yet*, she told herself, as Baby picked up the plate with both hands and licked it clean.

"Such a hungry boysie-woysie," Mrs Snicket said, with an adoring look. "And now, Baby dearest, why don't you have a little nap while I go upstairs and unpack?"

Baby burped loudly. "I can snooze here." He gave Mrs Moore a cold look. "And I don't want to be woken up, so no dusting or polishing or crashing the fire irons. *And* I want an extra cushion."

"Of course, my darling precious!" His doting mother picked up a cushion and tucked it tenderly behind his head.

Mrs Moore sniffed: she had herself been intending to have forty winks in her favourite chair. Only the thought of the neat little piles of shillings and sixpences on her office table kept her from dismissing Baby and his mother from her private parlour.

He'd better be good, she thought grimly, and went to the kitchen to talk to her cook.

Ten

WHILE ARABELLA WROTE OUT A NUMBER OF cards advertising Uncaster Hall as the ideal place for anyone seeking short term lodgings, Edie looked on admiringly.

"Cor! You do write lovely, Ma'am," she said. "Look at all them loops! Ever so smart, those are. That'll bring in the classy kind for sure. Keep the other sort away, too. Won't be able to make head nor tail of it."

Arabella inspected her handiwork; she found herself wondering if, perhaps, it did look a little too flowery.

Edie, however, was unstinting in her enthusiasm. "Lovely, they are. Really lovely! Give them to me and I'll run down to the high street right now this minute. There'll be people queuing up by this evening – just you wait and see!"

"I'll be happy if we have just one family," Arabella said. "Then I can get used to having lodgers gradually. I'm not sure quite how I'll feel about having strangers in my house..."

"You'll soon get used to it," Edie said cheerfully. "Trouble is, Ma'am, you ain't never had to share a bed with six little sisters. 'Spect you always had your own bed."

"I did once share with a cousin." Arabella sighed. "She kicked a lot."

"Terrible having a kicker." Edie was sympathetic. "Our Mattie, she was shocking. We used to put her at the end of the bed so we could push her out when she got too bad. But here's me rabbiting on when I should be down the town!"

Two minutes later she was hurrying out of the Hall, down the weed-infested drive, and into the long high street that boasted the majority of Uncaster's shops. She knew most of the shopkeepers well, and decided to visit those who were most likely to place a card in their window.

The Post Office was an obvious choice,

but Edie hesitated outside; the Post Officer was a gruff old man who could be difficult. *Come along, Edie*, she told herself. *Don't be such a scaredy cat! Mr Tramways can't eat you!* She took a deep breath and pushed open the door.

Mr Tramways was busy with a customer as Edie came in; a tall thin man was leaning over the counter, tapping his fingers in an irritable way. "The newspapers! Surely they should be here by now. The papers from York!"

"And I'm telling you they're not here yet, Mr Sleevery!" Mr Tramways's beard was bristling with indignation. "There's nothing come through but the *Uncaster Free Press*."

"Then give me one of those!" The man snatched up a copy and hurried out, almost knocking Edie over as he strode past her.

"That ain't no kind of gent!" she said indignantly. "Did you see that, Mr Tramways? Nearly pushed me into the wall!"

"Rude is what he is! Rude!" Mr Tramways was trembling with anger. "Comes in every day, and never a civil word! And me a representative of Her Majesty's Postal Service! Thinks he rules the world, just because he owns half the high street and twists poor folk out of their hard-earned pennies. Always wheeling and dealing, he is – and does he ever pay a fair price? Never. Buys cheap, sells dear. And if you don't pay your rent on time ... why, it's straight to the workhouse, and your house sold over your head. There's not many here as would have a good word to say for that one, however rich he may be."

Edie placed one of Arabella's elegantly written cards in front of the old man. "Would you be ever so kind, Mr Tramways, and pin this up somewhere? My Lady ... she's going to take in lodgers. Nice ones, of course."

Mr Tramways read the card with interest. "Lodgers, is it? I did hear there was trouble up at the Hall. That Honourable Henry ... I'd like to know what was honourable about him. What was he doing, fooling about on the top of a tower? Deserved what he got, by all accounts. And there's been a lot of folk talking about unpaid bills. Still, if Mrs Poskett is trying to pay them off, I'll not stand in her way. I'll put the card up Edie, and if anyone asks for lodgings I'll point them in the right direction."

Edie beamed her appreciation. "Thank you!" she said. "That'll be a real help! Everyone comes here sooner or later."

"And some more welcome than others." Mr Tramways frowned again, remembering his previous customer. "Now, was there anything else you were wanting? Because I've got accounts to see to."

Edie bobbed a grateful curtsey and left the Post Office to see if she could persuade Miss Twillfit in the milliners' shop to take a card. There were often notices in the window advertising second hand bonnets and capes – "Hardly Worn and at a Favourable Price!" – and Edie was hopeful.

Arriving at the little shop, she found Miss Twillfit lurking behind a shabbily dressed girl of about her own age, who was gazing wistfully at the ribbons. The milliner was obviously expecting her to snatch up a handful and run at any moment, and when she saw Edie her expression hardly altered. Edie, in her dirty dress and apron, was as suspect a customer as the girl in the patched and faded blue satin dress.

"Yes?" she said sharply. "Is it a message from

Mrs Poskett? You can tell her I'm not supplying as much as a neckerchief before my bill is paid! Months, I've been waiting... Months!"

Edie placed one of Arabella's cards on top of the ribbons; Miss Twillfit immediately snatched it up. "Don't go dirtying my stock, girl!" Curiosity made her glance at the card, and her eyebrows rose. "What's this? Lodgings? At Uncaster Hall? And what, pray, does the Honourable Henry have to say about that?"

"But, Miss Twillfit – hadn't you heard?" Edie was surprised. In Uncaster, news usually travelled from shop to shop with the speed of water flowing down a hill. "There was an accident, and Mr P – he's dead! Been dead a while now."

"Dead? Oh dear, oh dear. I can't say that I liked the man – much too hoity-toity in his ways – but *dead*? That's sad news." Miss Twillfit looked at the card again. "Especially for his poor, unfortunate wife. All right... I'll make an exception and take a card."

"Thank you, Miss," Edie smiled at the milliner – and then, on an impulse, turned to the girl standing beside the ribbon counter. "Here!

I ain't seen you in Uncaster before: take a card! You never know when you might be needing a place to sleep at night ... as the gravedigger said to the undertaker."

Rosie jumped. She had been dreaming of a new bonnet with scarlet ribbons, and had not paid much attention to the conversation. "Thanks," she said, "but me and the others, we'll be staying at The Golden Lion." She gave the ribbons a last wistful look. "I ought to be getting back there. They'll be wondering where I am."

"Take the card anyway," Edie told her. "You might meet someone who'd like it. Oh ... theatricals preferred!" And with a cheery smile at Rosie she trotted off to try her luck with the baker.

While Edie was out delivering her cards, Arabella was attempting to persuade her children to leave their rooms. The door was firmly locked so she was forced to call through the keyhole, at first with little result. All she could hear were squawks and cluckings, but at last Affogato came to the other side of the door. "What do you want?"

"Affy, my darling ... do come out and talk to me," his mother pleaded. "I'm sure we can find a way to make you and Hypatia happy."

"We told you, Mother!" Affogato was un-bending. "We want servants and horses and everything we had before!"

"But that's just not possible," Arabella told him. "Surely you can understand that? We've no money ... no money at all."

"And whose fault is that?" her son asked sourly. "It's certainly not ours."

Arabella began to defend herself, but Af-fogato ignored her and went on, "We've been talking, me and Hypatia. We were looking out of the window and we saw those horrible bailiff people riding up the drive, and we heard them talking about how everything's got to be sold ... so we've made a decision. We're going to go and live with Aunt Jocasta. She's got loads and loads of money, and she'll look after us PROPERLY!"

Her mother sat down on the floor in front of the keyhole. The Honourable Jocasta was the Honourable Henry's considerably older sister and a formidable old woman. She was indeed extremely rich, but had never shown any interest whatsoever in her nephew and niece. Obsessed with good breeding and the family name, she had refused to speak to Henry after his marriage to Arabella; indeed, she had sworn never to darken the door of Uncaster Hall again, even though it was where she had been born and brought up.

Cotton! she had exclaimed, her voice dripping with scorn. *Cotton! A TRADE connection! Henry Poskett ... you have brought shame and degradation to an old and distinguished family. From henceforth you are as dead to me. Do you hear me? DEAD!* And she had swept away in a flurry of velvet and satin, her aristocratic nose in the air.

Arabella, staring at the keyhole, found herself wondering if perhaps Affogato might be right. Maybe he and Hypatia would be happier with their aunt? She would be only too delighted to hear they had left their mother ... and, if Arabella was completely honest with herself, it was highly unlikely that the children would be of any assistance in her plan to take in lodgers.

"Affy darling," she said. "If you'd like to visit Aunt Jocasta, I'm sure I could write and ask her. Just come out, and we'll discuss it—"

There was a shifting of furniture, a mighty crash and a rattling of keys. A furious chicken screeched past Arabella's head, and Affogato and Hypatia appeared in the doorway, dressed in their outdoor clothes and each carrying a bulging bag.

"There's nothing to discuss, Mother," Hypatia said. "We're going. And we're going now this minute. We're taking that scraggy old horse, seeing as that's all you've left us with, and we'll tell Aunt Jocasta just how unutterably mean and horrible you are."

"That's right." Affogato nodded. "And you've only yourself to blame, Mother. If you'd been more careful with money, we wouldn't have to go! It's all your fault, you know." And without a backward glance they sailed down the stairs, leaving their mother speechless on the landing. A moment later Hypatia called up from the hallway, and for a brief second Arabella thought they had changed their minds – but it was only to inform her that a cupboard had fallen on one of the chickens, and it might be best to remove it before it spoilt the carpet.

"We'll send for the rest of our clothes as soon as we get there!" Hypatia added, then the front door slammed shut and Arabella sank her head in her hands.

When Edie came home an hour later, one of the chickens was roosting on top of the bust of the Honourable Henry's grandfather, and the others were wandering aimlessly round the hallway. She hooshed them out before going upstairs to see how they had escaped.

"Oh, Ma'am," she said when she saw Arabella. "Whatever's happened?"

Arabella looked up. "They've gone, Edie. Gone to their aunt's house ... and I can't blame them. Everything they're used to has vanished and I really don't see how I'm ever going to get it back again."

Edie, who had formed her own opinion of Hypatia and Affogato, sat down beside her employer. "It'll be all right, Ma'am. It's always blackest before dawn, my Gran used to say ... and I've put lots of your cards out in the town. Mr Tramways, he was ever so nice about it! Said as he'd send people here for sure."

Arabella sighed. Edie's never-failing cheerfulness was, without a doubt, a blessing ... but just at the moment, everything seemed unremittingly dark. She roused herself a little to tell Edie about the unfortunate chicken in Hypatia's bedroom, and was astonished to see the little kitchen maid's face light up.

"Goodness me, Ma'am! Every cloud has a silver lining! We'll have roast chicken tonight, and that'll make you feel ever so much better. There's potatoes in the garden and cabbage too ... it'll be a feast fit for a queen!" And with a beaming smile, Edie hurried to move the cupboard and collect that night's dinner.

Eleven

ROSIE, ON REACHING THE GOLDEN LION, WAS surprised to find her family sitting outside. The wicker hampers had been put in a shed behind the small stage, but they were surrounded by their personal luggage. A sense of gloom hung over them. Even Pa Pringle had a despondent air about him, but he stood up to give Rosie a hug. "There you are, beloved daughter mine! I was beginning to fear you were lost – lost in the cold and unfeeling wilderness that is Uncaster!"

Aunt Mags sniffed. "I'd call it plain unfriendly."

Gertie and Vinnie nodded their agreement; Charlie made a face at his sister. "They don't want us staying at The Golden Lion. We've got to find somewhere else, and it's all because we're not called the 'Pringle Players' any more."

"Ridiculous!" Gertie folded her arms. "If we didn't need the work, I'd have given that stupid landlord a piece of my mind."

"So here we are." Pa threw out his arms to embrace the cruel world. "Homeless upon a blasted heath. 'Blow, winds, and crack—'"

"But we can stay here!" Rosie was struggling to pull Arabella's card out of her pocket. "Look! I met a girl and she gave me this – and she said 'theatricals preferred'!"

There was a stunned silence before Pa picked Rosie up and swung her round in triumph. "Behold our saviour!"

The Noble Hero studied the card with interest. "Fancy writing," he said approvingly. "And a hall, too!"

Pa put Rosie down. "A hall? What kind of hall? Music? Church? Village? You get terrible draughts in a village hall... My rheumatics can't cope."

"Uncaster Hall," Vinnie said. "Look!"

"That'll be pricey," Aunt Mags declared. "Bound to be. Can't think why they'd want us."

"But they do," Rosie said. "And the girl I met – she wasn't at all smart! She was nice and ordinary, and she had smuts all over her face."

"Hmmm..." Pa considered. "Well ... I suppose it wouldn't hurt to go and have a look."

Vinnie picked up a bag. "And we can't sit here all night."

And so it was agreed – the Steam Whistle Theatre Company picked up their belongings and set off. Stopping at the Post Office to ask the way, they were encouraged to see another card tucked in the window and Mr Tramways was happy to give them directions. "Straight down to the end of the street," he told them. "Big rusty gates ... seen better days. You can't miss it."

Pa Pringle bowed. "Thank you, dear Sir. And may I invite you to visit us at The Golden Lion? I can promise you an edifying evening with the works of the noble Bard!"

Mr Tramways scratched his whiskery chin. "Don't know as I hold with the nobility," he said. "That Honourable Henry – he was good for nothing but debts, that's why his poor

95

lady's taking in lodgers. No... Count me out on that one."

Seeing Pa struggle with this remark, Aunt Mags took his arm. "We'd best be on our way. Thank you for your help. Come along, Fred!"

It wasn't long before the gates of Uncaster Hall came into view. Aunt Mags was heartened by their dilapidated state and revised her gloomy expectations of an extortionate rent. She was even more pleased to discover that the Hall was not the enormous building she had expected. "Not much more than a big house," she said, and counted the windows. "Hmmm. Eight bedrooms at most, I'd say. Wouldn't be much to talk about in London and that's the truth."

Charlie and Rosie ran ahead and hopped their way up and down the stone steps, before going back to bang on the knocker. Edie opened the door, and when she saw Rosie her face lit up. "Oh! It's you! I'm ever so glad. Is this your family?"

Pa stepped forward, but Aunt Mags, feeling she had had quite enough of her brother playing the grand impresario, pushed her way in front. "Good evening, my dear. We're looking for lodgings for three or four weeks ... would that be possible, do you think?"

Edie's smile was ecstatic. "Six of you? Oh YES! Come in, I'll run and fetch my lady." Then, remembering her own advice, she put on a serious expression. "Terms to be arranged, of course." With another quick smile at Rosie, she ran off down the corridor to find Arabella.

"Ooooh! I can smell roast chicken!" Charlie was sniffing the air and rubbing his stomach. Rosie, who hadn't thought about food since leaving London, suddenly realised how very hungry she was.

"Do we get food as well as beds?" she asked hopefully.

Aunt Mags shrugged. "Depends on the terms," she said.

The Canary of Covent Garden was also hungry. "I say we ask for full board," she said. "Works out easier in the long run. What do you think, Vinnie?"

Vinnie nodded. "Sounds sensible to me. Hey!

Is that our landlady?" He patted his hair into place and gazed admiringly at Arabella as she came swooping towards them, followed by Edie.

Pa elbowed Aunt Mags aside, and made his most theatrical bow. "May I present myself and my humble company, Madam: the Steam Whistle Theatre Company. Honoured to be here, in your illustrious home."

"Thank you." Arabella dropped such a gracious curtsey that Rosie made a mental note to copy it at the first opportunity. "You're very welcome."

Behind her, Edie hissed, "*Terms*, Ma'am! Ask them what they're thinking of paying!"

"Oh ... yes. Of course." Arabella blushed. Discussing money was something she had seldom had to do before; she gave Edie an agonized look. "Edie, dear – perhaps you could..."

Edie, recognizing Aunt Mags as the financial brains of the party, turned to her. "What was you thinking of paying, Miss? We've got three rooms ready, if the little 'uns don't mind sharing. And would you be wanting full board, 'cos that's extra – but we ain't as grand as we look. It'll be plain enough."

Aunt Mags considered. There was a steely look in Edie's eyes that she couldn't help but admire, but she was used to bargaining and relished a good fight. "We couldn't possibly pay more than a shilling a week," she declared.

Arabella looked baffled: was this good? It didn't sound very much. But Edie, who had anticipated a low offer, saw her opportunity. "A shilling, Miss? You mean a shilling a week per room? And you'll be wanting three rooms? That'll be three shillings a week, and another three for board. Six shillings a week, Miss, all in."

Aunt Mags, who thought anything over four shillings a week for full board was daylight robbery, bristled – but before she could make a counter offer, she was undermined by Pa. He bowed again to Arabella before striking the bent and shaking pose of an ancient man. "'If money go before, all ways do lie open.' Polonius spoke well: wise, wise words indeed. Madam, we are indebted to you for your generosity."

Aunt Mags was forced to contain her silent fury as Pa placed six silver shillings in Edie's small and dirty hand; six shillings that Aunt

Mags knew left them with nothing but a few half-pennies.

"Ta ever so," Edie said, as she transferred the money to her pocket. "And now I'd best run, or the chicken'll be burnt to a cinder!"

As she disappeared, Arabella smiled at Pa. "Do please follow me to the drawing room," she said. "Dinner will be ready soon."

Aunt Mags, still resenting the six shillings, coughed loudly. "I'd like to see the rooms first, if you don't mind. I need to check them out, make sure they're worth it."

Arabella was unfazed by this rudeness. "Of course," she said. "That was thoughtless of me!" And she led the way up the wide oak staircase. The Steam Whistle Theatre Company trailed after her, Aunt Mags looking suspiciously at the holes in the carpet. "Watch out for damp!" she hissed at Gertie. "These old places ... bound to have a leaking roof!"

There were, however, no leaks. The bed hangings and furniture were old and well worn, but the rooms were spacious. Rosie was delighted to find a large four poster bed with heavy velvet drapes.

"It's just like a little theatre! I love it!" she said. Even the thought of Aunt Mags snoring on the other side of the bolster wasn't a depressant: she and Charlie, who had a truckle bed in the corner, unpacked their belongings with enthusiasm.

"I like it too," Charlie agreed. "Are you ready? I'm starving!"

Hurrying downstairs, it took them a moment or two to locate the kitchen. Edie, after consultation with Arabella, had decided it would be easier all round if the grand dining room was abandoned and the kitchen became the centre of activities.

"We ain't got too much coal left," she explained, "and without a fire, that there dining room is as chilly as my grandma's grave. The kitchen's nice and cozy, though."

Arabella, well aware that the coal merchant's bill was sitting unpaid on the table in her room, was happy to agree. When Pa Pringle appeared, she asked if he would be kind enough to sit at the head of the table and wield the carving knife. Pa, delighted at this patrician role, agreed with enthusiasm.

"'Mine eyes smell onions; I shall weep anon.'" He gave gusty sigh. "How wonderful is William!"

"William?" Arabella looked puzzled and Aunt Mags, who had taken it upon herself to hand round the vegetables, shook her head.

"He means Shakespeare," she explained. "I'm afraid you'll hear a lot of that."

Arabella smiled. "Oh, of course! How silly of me. I'm very fond of *A Midsummer Night's Dream*, myself."

Rosie kicked Charlie under the table. Puck was a role that he hated, but was forced to play; it was almost inevitable that Pa would ask him to recite for Arabella's benefit.

Fortunately, Edie came staggering in with a huge dish of boiled potatoes and Charlie was spared. "I'm ever so sorry, folks," she said. "I've done extra spuds, but there ain't nothing more after this." She looked at Arabella. "Did you tell them we're pretty nearly bust, Ma'am?" She dumped the potatoes on the table with a crash. "Ain't no use pretending otherwise."

Aunt Mags looked pleased rather than disappointed. "We're used to plain food." And then, scenting the possibility of a late victory, she rose from her chair. "Supposing we help with the chores? Gertie's a dab hand at bread and pastry, aren't you, Gertie? Of course we'd expect a small reduction in the rent. Suppose we pay four shillings a week, all in?"

Edie's snort was worthy of Aunt Mags herself. "Couldn't do it for less than five and six, Miss."

"Five, and that's my last word." Aunt Mags folded her arms.

For the first time Edie's gaze wavered. "Oh, Miss ... I'm so sorry, but we really needs the money as well as the help. There's all the sheets and undies to wash, you see, as well as putting food on the table and saving a little bit for bills, and there's only me to do it..." She pushed a wisp of hair away. "But if that's your last offer..."

Aunt Mags, who had never yet let a landlady get the better of her, looked at Edie's peaky little face for a long moment. Charlie and Rosie held their breath.

"We'll pay the six shillings," she said gruffly. "And we'll help with the chores. And the washing."

"Cor blimey!" Edie was glowing. "Thanks ever so much, Miss! I'll remember this, swear to God and hope to die! You're a good 'un, Miss, and no mistake. Anything I can ever do for you, just you ask – as the magpie said to the cheesemonger."

It wasn't often that anyone paid Aunt Mags a compliment. She gave Edie an embarrassed nod and cleared her throat. "Yes. Well. Thank you ... *ahem*. Isn't it time we sat down to eat this splendid meal? And when we've finished—" she turned to Charlie— "why don't we send you and Rosie out to have a look round? See how busy The Golden Lion is in the evenings."

Arabella had been listening to Edie bargaining with Aunt Mags with astonished admiration. She leant forward with a suggestion: "Why don't you take Edie with you? She's been working non-stop all day."

Charlie and Rosie agreed with enthusiasm, but Edie hesitated. "There's going to be an awful lot of dishes to clear and wash, Ma'am."

Aunt Mags looked noble. "A woman's work is never done! Gertie and I can see to the dishes, can't we, Gertie?"

When Gertie nodded, Edie dropped her a curtsey. "Thank you, Miss! Thank you, Ma'am! Thanks EVER so much!"

Twenty minutes later the three children bounced down the steps of Uncaster Hall, delighted to be out in the evening air.

Twelve

IT WAS A BEAUTIFUL SUMMER'S EVENING AND only just beginning to get dark as Charlie hopped his way down the drive, whistling happily. Rosie and Edie hopped behind him, chatting as they went.

"Why's Mrs Poskett letting out rooms?" Rosie asked. "She isn't like the usual landladies we meet. Not at all!"

"She's a lovely lady." Edie nodded several times for emphasis. "And she's had ever such a hard life. Those kids of hers ... they're so spoilt, I wouldn't serve them up in a sweet shop. And as for that husband – he was as rotten as a mouldy plum. Even a worm would turn its nose up at the Honourable Henry, and that's a fact ... but she's solid gold."

The three of them linked arms as they walked up the high street, Charlie and Rosie inspecting everything with interest. Even though this was the most important road in Uncaster, it wasn't nearly as wide as the streets they were used to. Most of the traffic consisted of farm wagons, or delivery carts, or riders on stubby little ponies. There were no grand carriages and no high-stepping thoroughbreds. The shops and stalls were small as well; many had bow-windows with tiny diamond panes of glass that twinkled and winked in the evening light.

Rosie wanted to look in each one, but Charlie pulled her past. "We'll never get to The Golden Lion if you're so slow," he said. "Come on!"

Edie squeezed Rosie's hand. "I'll show you the bestest ones another time," she promised.

Rosie gave a little skip. "I like it here! It smells much nicer than London. Don't you think so, Charlie?"

He gave an exploratory sniff. "Maybe." Then he noticed the poster:

MRS MOORE'S SUPPER ROOMS
UNCASTER

GREAT SUCCESS!
CROWDED HOUSES!
EXCLUSIVE!

LITTLE BABY
BUBBLES!
THE World-Famous
Child Magician
AND Escapologist

ONLY TO BE SEEN AT
MRS MOORE'S SUPPER ROOMS
GRAND OPENING AT
7.30PM ON 5TH JUNE

Charlie grew thoughtful. "An evening performance," he said. "That'll be direct competition with us. And we haven't got a single poster up yet!"

"Do you do magic too?" Edie asked.

Charlie looked shocked. "We're a theatre company. We do plays! Shakespeare, and lots of other things." He saw Edie's puzzled expression. "You do know who Shakespeare is, don't you?"

"Is he the guy you calls 'Pa'?" Edie asked. "Or the other one ... the one with no teeth?"

"Shakespeare lived ages and ages ago," Rosie explained, "and he wrote lots of plays. Pa rewrites bits sometimes, but he keeps the stories the same – well, almost..."

Edie was still puzzled. "If he's dead, why do you do his plays?"

Charlie jumped onto a step, and threw out his arms in imitation of Pa Pringle. "'Shakespeare,'" he boomed, "'was the finest playwright who ever lived, and his words live on and on in the mouths of the Steam Whistle Theatre Company!'"

"On and on and ON," Rosie agreed. "Pa's

always quoting them. Ma says it's difficult to get him to talk proper English."

"Proper English?" Charlie slapped his forehead in mock horror. "The words of our noble Bard are far more proper than any we have nowadays, fair lady."

"You do that kind of talking ever so well," Edie said admiringly, and she looked at Rosie. "Can you do it too?"

Rosie clasped her hands and flung herself at Edie's feet. "'My Lord Augustus, pray heed the pleas of a poor and miserable orphan! I am nothing to you, I know, but have pity – oh, have pity on a poor defenceless girl who has no friend to care for her ... no family to protect her ... and not a single companion to speak for her!'"

For a moment, Edie was speechless. There were tears in her eyes – she brushed them away with a grubby sleeve. "Cor, Rosie... That was... That was just the most BEAUTIFUL words I ever did hear!"

"Shame she doesn't do it as well as that when she's on stage," Charlie said, and as Rosie jumped up to punch him he danced away beyond her reach. "Hey, Edie – where's this Supper Rooms place? Are we near?"

Edie shook herself back into the real world. "The Supper Rooms? There they are, just across the road. They don't open on a Monday. *Ooooh*... Look at all them posters!"

They were hard to miss: Mrs Moore had given Jago his instructions, and the entire front wall was plastered with pictures of Little Baby Bubbles ... a rather younger and slimmer Baby Bubbles than the one currently fast asleep in Mrs Moore's favourite armchair.

Charlie, Rosie and Edie considered the posters. "He don't look too happy," Edie said at last. "Tied up in knots like that."

"I thought it would be a real baby." Rosie was disappointed. "He looks almost as old as we are."

"He wouldn't be able to do tricks if he was a real baby," Charlie said scornfully. "It's just show-talk, like our Vinnie: the 'Noble Hero'."

As they stood looking, the door to the Supper Rooms opened and Jago, the kitchen boy, came out carrying a bucket. He saw Edie and stuck out his tongue. *"Yer!"* he jeered. "Workhouse girl! Run away from your stinking pit, have you? Workhouse, workhouse! Bet your ma was no better than she should be!"

"Oi!" Charlie was over the road in an instant. "That's my friend you're talking to! Say you're sorry!"

"*Oooo-er!* Gone and got yourself a beau, have you, Edie? Bet he doesn't know you workhouse kids have fleas and worms and ever so much worse!" And with the slithering action of an eel, Jago was out of Charlie's reach and running down the road.

"Next time I see that boy," Charlie said angrily, "I'll punch his nose!"

Edie shook her head. "Won't do any good, but ta for the offer. He's a bad 'un. Never stops sneaking and spying and causing trouble. Even if you did punch his nose, he'd only go weeping and screaming to Mrs Moore saying he wasn't doing nothing when the nasty boy came and hit him – and then it'd be *you* in trouble." She gave the Supper Rooms one last glance. "Do you want us to tear them posters down before we go?"

"Tear them down? NO!" Charlie was horrified.

"We mustn't ever do anything like that," said Rosie. "We show-people look out for each other, even if we don't like each other much. We get enough aggravation from folks outside, without bringing it on ourselves."

"Sorry." Edie drooped. "I thought it might help."

Rosie smiled at her. "It's all right. A few companies do rip up each other's posters, but it makes them ever so unpopular. You get horrible fights and all sorts."

"Oh..." Edie was thinking she had a lot to learn. "Are you going to put posters up, too?"

"We'll be out early in the morning," Charlie said. "We'll probably open the day after, so's not to clash. Better not to split an audience in two."

"Do you think Pa'll let us come and see the magician?" Rosie asked.

Charlie grinned. "Hope so. We need to see what we're up against!"

The Golden Lion, unlike the Supper Rooms, was very definitely open. The sound of raucous singing could be heard from some way away, and Rosie gave Charlie an anxious glance. "It sounds just like The Dog and Duck, Charlie ... and they hated us there."

Charlie looked at Edie. "Is it always this noisy?"

Edie rubbed her nose. "Cook – she wouldn't let any of us younger ones come here. She said it weren't suitable... She said – excuse me, Miss – she said the blokes as come here get as tiddly as a pondful of newts."

"Did your Cook ever come and see a play here?" Rosie wanted to know, and Edie went pink and looked at her feet.

"I only knows that one time they had dancing girls. Cook said it was the most terrible thing she ever did see! She said they didn't hardly have any clothes on, Miss, and they threw their legs about something dreadful."

This made Charlie laugh, but Rosie was shocked. "Oh no ... Pa won't like that." She stopped. "Listen ... they're not singing any-more!"

A moment later, it became all too obvious that a fight had broken out. There were various crashes, thuds, and a lot of angry shouting, followed by a moment's relative silence before the singing began again – even louder.

Charlie made a face at Rosie and Edie. "Maybe we won't go any closer. Let's hurry back and tell Pa."

Once Charlie, Rosie and Edie had trailed back to Uncaster Hall, they found Pa, Aunt Mags and Vinnie deep in discussion about the Steam Whistle Theatre Company's opening production. The Canary of Covent Garden had gone to her nest with a headache and Arabella, pleading exhaustion, had also retired to bed.

Pa was extolling the virtues of his version of *King Lear* as the children walked in. He greeted them with a booming, "Heyday and holiday! My dears, how didst thou fare?"

Edie's eyes opened wide and she tugged at Charlie's arm. "Is he talking that play-talk?" she whispered.

Charlie nodded. "Yes," and then, "Pa, you're not going to like this much... The Golden Lion's exactly like The Dog and Duck."

"Worse," Rosie said. "They were singing so loudly we could hear them streets away, and then they had a terrible fight, and we could hear them shouting and screaming, and then they started singing again..."

"And the Supper Rooms' walls are covered in posters for Baby Bubbles' magic show." Charlie took up the story. "And there's posters all up and down the high street. It's closed tonight, but it looks much classier than the Lion. Couldn't we play there instead?"

Pa was shocked by this suggestion. "No, Charlie! No! The Supper Rooms have their own show, and The Golden Lion awaits our coming. You said there was singing? Music, sweet music, is everything. And a rousing chorus by men of the earth suggests enthusiasm to me: enthusiasm for the finer things of life. Enthusiasm for us, for drama, for the works of William Shakespeare!" He puffed out his chest and stuck his thumbs in his waistcoat. "*King Lear*, I think. The glory and the majesty of Lear ... that alone will satisfy the hungry souls of the good people of Uncaster."

"But, Pa..." Rosie began.

Pa waved her into silence. "But me no buts, Rosie! The die is cast, the word is spoken. To-morrow, we will rehearse."

When Pa Pringle was in this mood, there was no point in arguing. Rosie rolled her eyes at Charlie and Edie, and gave up. "I'm going to bed," she said.

Edie, who had understood very little of Pa's speech, saw that Rosie was upset. "I'll fetch you a candle, Miss," she said. "And one of them naughty hens has laid an egg on the doormat, so you can have that for your breakfast."

Rosie gave her a grateful look. "Thank you, Edie… but you have to call me Rosie! We're friends, aren't we?"

"*Ooooh* yes, Miss – I mean, Rosie." Edie beamed, and Charlie smiled back at her.

"And me," he said. "We're friends too, so call me Charlie."

This was almost too much for Edie. She hurried out to fetch the candles and, after Rosie and Charlie had gone upstairs, went singing to the dark little cupboard where she slept.

"Cor blimey," she said, as she shook out her moth-eaten blanket. "If only my gran could've heard that! Edie Boiler has two friends what does play acting. Stone the blooming crows…"

Thirteen

OLIO SLEEVERY WAS UP EARLY. HE HEADED straight for the Post Office, only to discover Mr Tramways had not yet opened the door. Olio grunted irritably, but Arabella's card caught his attention and he bent down to read it.

"Letting rooms, is she? *Hmmm* ... that's a big house. A *very* big house." His cold grey eyes gleamed as he pulled the previous day's paper out of his pocket and ran his finger down the advertisements – several of which were marked. "An investor is looking for a large property in Uncaster. Condition is immaterial. Funds available, up to nine hundred pounds ... interesting. Very interesting!"

When Mr Tramways arrived, Olio greeted him with a chilly smile. "Good morning. My newspapers, if you please."

Mr Tramways pulled a packet from under the counter. "Came from York last night."

As he took them Olio said casually, "So Mrs Poskett's turned landlady. Bad debts, I presume."

"None of my business," Mr Tramways said shortly.

Olio, noting he had not been contradicted, was satisfied. He put the papers in his case, walked out of the Post Office, and headed for Uncaster Hall. The overgrown drive pleased him, as did the evident lack of upkeep. Taking care to avoid the windows he walked slowly round the building, inspecting the peeling paint and crumbling brickwork.

"No money there," he told himself. "Excellent. And lodgers? Won't pay enough to put it back in order." He stroked his chin as he walked away. "Now ... how to persuade her to sell?"

A thought came to him and he headed up the high street to the ironmonger's shop. The owner, a small wizened woman, was a useful gossip: she had in the past pointed Olio towards homes where families were struggling to make ends meet. The offer of silver shillings for their sad little houses, with a promise they could continue as tenants, was met with blessings and profound relief ... it was usually at least three months before Olio had the families evicted, and the house sold on at a profit.

The ironmonger was suitably rewarded. She, like Olio, had no scruples; she was as unrelenting as the gleaming brass door handles in her shop window. If she was pleased to see Olio Sleevery she did not show it – she invited him inside with a twitch of her shoulder. His enquiry about Arabella's finances, however, made her cackle.

"Butcher, baker, wine merchant ... they're all owed. Sent the bailiffs in, didn't they? Serves her right. Nobody don't deserve a great big house like that unless they worked for it. And has she ever lifted a finger? Ha! Not her! But she'll be in the gutter before long ... just you wait."

Another half-hour and Olio had all the information he needed.

Eliza Snicket was also up early. After some thought, she had decided it was unlikely that the Steam Whistle Theatre Company had heard anything about her past history. Nevertheless, word might yet reach them – so it would be better if she could blacken their reputation before they had a chance to blacken hers. Suspecting that she might have a useful ally in the weasel-eyed Jago, she went downstairs to find him.

Discovering him in the kitchen, she smiled sweetly. "What a handsome young man you are, Jago! I'm sure the Uncaster girls all adore you … I know that if I were younger I'd be fluttering my eyelashes and hoping you'd notice me."

Jago, half-flattered, half-suspicious, peered at Baby's mother. "What d'you want, Missus?"

Mrs Snicket's smile grew sweeter still. "Want? Me? Nothing! Well … perhaps for you to think of me as a friend. Do you think you could do that, Jago dear?"

"Dunno." Jago squinted at her. "What's in it for me?"

"Oh, you naughty, naughty boy!" She gave a trill of laughter. "How sensible you are to look after yourself. I wish my darling Baby was like you – but he's an artist, and his dear little head is filled with magic."

Jago remained unmoved and Mrs Snicket leant closer so she could whisper. "It's always so useful to have a sharp pair of eyes and ears! Especially if they're checking to see what a common little theatre company from London is up to at The Golden Lion."

This suggestion appealed to Jago. His nose quivered, but he showed no other sign of enthusiasm as he said, "It'll cost you, Missus. I don't do other people's dirty work for nothing."

"Dirty work?" Eliza Snicket laughed a merry laugh. "Now, now, Jago! What a thing to say! And of course I was thinking of presenting you with a token of my gratitude—"

"Don't want no tokens," Jago growled. "Shilling a day. That's my terms. Take it or leave it." He shrugged. "Ain't no skin off my nose if the Lion has theatricals." A thought came to him, and for the first time he brightened. "Hey! Ain't those high-kicking girls, is it?"

"You'll have to go and see." Mrs Snicket told him. "And I'll give you sixpence – but only if *you* give *me* a full report."

Jago had been about to argue for an increase, but was interrupted by Mrs Moore appearing in the doorway. "What are you doing here?" she said sharply. "I asked you to collect the fish ten minutes ago!"

"Just going, Mrs Moore!" Jago picked up a straw basket and slid away.

Leaving the Supper Rooms he sped up the high street towards the fishmonger's stall, thinking as he went. He had no intention of helping Mrs Snicket spy on her competition, until he had established a proper rate of payment. But, as he was within a stone's throw of The Golden Lion, it occurred to him that he could see if it was indeed a return visit by Madame Virginia Vestibule's Delicious Dancing Delights.

He swerved away from the High Street into Marshall Lane ... and stopped dead.

Outside the Lion was a poster celebrating the arrival of the Steam Whistle Theatre Company, and a small group of adults and children were standing beside it, checking it was pasted firmly onto the wall. A moment later they opened the door to go in, and Jago recognized Charlie and Rosie.

He gave a low whistle as he stared, eyes narrowed, at Charlie's departing back. *So Edie's beau's part of the theatre company*, he said to himself. *Well, well, well. In that case, I'll work for sixpence a day and be glad to do it!*

Charlie had threatened to attack him and, what was worse, had threatened to attack him in defense of Edie, a creature Jago despised. Whether he despised her because of her workhouse background or because she had always refused to speak to him was not something Jago had ever chosen to think about. All he knew was that every time he saw her he wanted to grind her into the dust: vicious retribution was his trademark, and his memory for slights and insults was long.

"I'll get you both," he muttered. "Teach you a proper lesson, I will. Workhouse dregs and theatre scum ... just you wait!"

Then, deciding he didn't dare keep Mrs Moore waiting any longer for her fish, he hurried off.

Inside the yard of The Golden Lion, Pa was studying the stage. It was small but sturdy;

tall poles at each corner supported a high rail where curtains could be hung.

"Excellent," he declared. "I could have wished for gaslight, but the summer is here and the evenings bright." He swung round and inspected the yard. "And plenty of room for our audience ... an audience who will hang on our every word. Truly, my friends, we have done well!"

Aunt Mags was not so convinced. There was a strong smell of stale beer, and the shrubs and plants had been trampled into the muddy ground. There were shards of broken flower pots swept against the walls. Remembering Rosie's report of the night before, Aunt Mags wondered if Pa was, as usual, being overly optimistic in his enthusiasm.

"We'll see what we see when we see it," she said. "So we're really opening tomorrow night?"

Pa nodded. "Today we'll set the stage: curtains, props, and scenery. And we'll have one last rehearsal, in order to speak the speech trippingly upon the tongue – and not falter or stutter in the telling of the tale of Lear, King of Kings."

Aunt Mags looked doubtful. "And leave everything out here overnight?"

"Have faith, Margaretta!" Pa was shocked. "I shall, of course, speak to our host and ask that his merry customers are kind and gentle with our possessions."

Vinnie groaned. "Honestly, Fred! Kind and gentle? Use your eyes, man! This is a tavern! Look what they've done to the flower pots!"

"Mere youthful exuberance," Pa said, but he sounded hopeful rather than certain.

Rosie, who had been sent with Charlie to fetch the hampers out of the shed, came hurrying round the back of the stage, holding her nose. "Pa! There's a man asleep in the costume basket and he's been sick!"

"Ha!" Her worst suspicions confirmed, Aunt Mags went to do battle.

Two minutes later, a bleary-eyed man staggered into the yard, patted Charlie on the head and told him he was a "dear little laddie ... just like my dear little laddie at home", before zigzagging his way into the bar.

Aunt Mags reappeared, her face grim. "We'll not be opening tomorrow, Fred. It'll take me and Gertie a couple of days at the very least to wash and dry the curtains and the costumes – unless you want to play Lear stark naked!"

Gertie gave a sour laugh. "That'd certainly make up for the fact we haven't got any dancing girls."

"It might not be a bad idea to hold off opening for a bit, you know," Vinnie said thoughtfully. "If this baby magician's any good, he'll bring in the crowds for at least three or four days ... and we can use the time to build up expectation. We can get some flyers printed, and Rosie and Charlie can hand them out... Maybe we could offer a special price for booking in advance – that way we'd know what kind of interest there was."

"And that would give us some money." Aunt Mags' forehead was furrowed as she considered Vinnie's suggestion. "We've got to find another six shillings for rent in a week's time. That poor Poskett woman can't afford to carry us for even a couple of days. But I don't think you'll find a printer willing to give us flyers for love; we'll have to pay for those." She paused. "I don't think we've got much choice. We might manage without a few of the costumes, but we certainly need the curtains ... and they'll be in no fit state unless they're washed. What do you think, Fred?"

Pa Pringle held out his arms to the Noble Hero. "Dear Vincent – I applaud your genius and I bow to your wisdom. We will do as you suggest."

As Vinnie suffered Pa's congratulatory hug with a roll of the eyes, Gertie made a suggestion: "What about asking the Supper Rooms if they'd let me do a song before the magician comes on? Kind of a prologue ... just for this week? There's my new song about magic – it'd set the mood just right, and it'd bring in a little money."

Pa coughed loudly. "Just what I was going to suggest," he said, "and our wonderful songbird can use the moment to remind the crowds that high drama will be taking place at The Golden Lion very shortly. Anticipation is all!"

Fourteen

Pa AND GERTIE WENT TOGETHER TO THE Supper Rooms to discuss their proposition. Mrs Moore fought hard against the idea of paying more than a shilling a week, and refused to allow Gertie to advertise the Steam Whistle Theatre Company: that, she said, would be ridiculous. She had no desire whatsoever to encourage competition, and if that was why they had come she would *immediately* withdraw her permission for an opening act.

Pa was about to admit defeat, but Gertie, who knew that even a shilling would come in handy, said she would accept the terms offered. "I have a delightful song called 'Life of Magic'," she explained. "It's topping the bill in London. I'm sure you've heard of it?"

Mrs Moore hadn't, but would never have admitted as much. "I'll expect you tomorrow evening at half past seven," she said. "Don't be late."

Eliza Snicket was pleased when she heard the news.

"An opening act for my precious boy!" she cooed. "And from Covent Garden, too. Of course, he's more than used to celebrities wishing to share a stage with him. It happened all the time in London."

She was less pleased when she realised Gertie was a member of the Steam Whistle Theatre Company, soon to perform at The Golden Lion. "Dearest Mrs Moore, do tell!" she said. "What kind of place is The Golden Lion? Do they often have theatre companies there?"

Mrs Moore shrugged. "They've never had one before – they don't go in for entertainment. Not what *I'd* call entertainment, anyway." She lowered her voice. "They did have dancing girls there once. Disgusting!"

Determined that Baby was going to be the

star of Uncaster for many weeks to come – or at least until her funds were sufficiently restored to allow them to move on with comfort – Mrs Snicket was delighted. A venue that hosted dancing girls was unlikely to attract a respectable theatre company. Nevertheless, it was best to be careful.

When Baby went for his morning nap, exhausted after eating his way through a plate piled high with devilled kidneys, rashers of bacon, slices of beef and several pork chops, his mother sidled down to the kitchen where Jago was grumpily gutting fish.

"My dear friend," she began, with a beaming smile.

Jago waved a fishy knife in response. "Ain't nobody's 'dear friend'. And I want sixpence."

Mrs Snicket, noting with satisfaction that he had accepted her offer, fished in her capacious bag and produced a sixpence. Jago bit it to make sure it was genuine, then dropped it into the pocket of his apron. "So? What d'you want now?"

"Well…" Mrs Snicket pretended to consider. "The thing is, my friend, that it's very important for my sweet boy to do well. Another entertainment, however terrible it might be, will harm him—"

"You mean it'll cut the cash," Jago said, and sliced a herring in half with a swoop of his knife.

"Exactly! What a brain you have. So, any tiny titbits of news that you can bring me, or any little interruptions you might see fit to put in their way..." Mrs Snicket let her sentence hang unfinished in the air.

Jago whistled through his teeth. "Damage to property? That'll be extra. That's dangerous stuff, Missus."

"Damage?" Mrs Snicket's eyes widened. "Did I use the word, damage? I think not!"

"Interruptions, damage – where's the difference?" Jago dismembered another fish. Grudgingly, he added, "Took your sixpence, didn't I? So you'll just have to wait and see. But now I got fish to gut, so I ain't got time to talk."

And with that, Mrs Snicket had to be satisfied. Not wanting to get in Mrs Moore's way, she decided to make sure that Baby's black box was in place, and all the equipment for his magic tricks arranged in the right order.

The supper room was large, with as many tables and benches as Mrs Moore could squeeze in. Her predecessor had built a small platform as a stage, and in order to raise the tone of her entertainments she had set up curtains. Sometimes, when they became so splashed with beer that she was obliged to take them down and wash them, she felt they were a mistake. But on other occasions she enjoyed the drama of pulling them back to reveal the star of the evening.

Mrs Snicket inspected the room with interest. It was larger than she had expected; she guessed that at least 40 people could be seated at the tables. As she had negotiated a 50:50 split on the takings with Mrs Moore, she immediately began to make her calculations.

Just as long as darling Baby is a success, she thought, *we should earn enough to set up in York by the end of the month...*

When all the various boxes, bowls and trick containers were where they should be, she went to arrange the chains Baby would escape from at the end of his performance, neatly coiling them in a corner. Then, after glancing round to make sure she was alone, she opened her bag and began to count her money. For someone who had claimed to be nearly penniless her purse was remarkably heavy. Mrs Moore would have been interested to see how many sixpences it contained, and the sailor from the train might have wondered how his two golden sovereigns came to be part of her collection.

Little Baby Bubbles was not the only one to have mastered sleight of hand.

A sound disturbed her, and Mrs Snicket closed her bag with a snap as Baby made his way over, yawning. "Dearest boy! Have you had a lovely sleep?"

"No." Baby looked round the Supper Rooms. "Couldn't you have found a proper theatre? I don't like this place, it smells of old stew."

His mother suppressed a sigh. It was important to keep him happy: a disgruntled Baby meant a poor performance. "Darling boysie-woysie ... this is just a beginning!" She decided a lie might help the situation, and put her finger to her lips. "My sweet, I'll tell you a little secret. There's a man from a really, really big music hall slipping in to see you.

It might be tonight, or it might be tomorrow or the next day, and if he likes what he sees – and, my darling, of course he will – then he'll ask you to be his star!"

"You're telling fibs." Baby glowered. "I know you are. You're just trying to get me to work in this stupid place."

Mrs Snicket gave a trill of laughter. "Oh, Baby dearest! How could you even think such a thing?"

"Because you're as crooked as a bent nail." Baby had another look round. "Why would anyone from a music hall come here?"

There was a faint doubt in his voice, and Mrs Snicket seized her chance. "Why do you think, precious one? To see my darling Baby Bubbles, of course! He thinks you'd be perfect to top the bill!"

Baby was torn between wanting to believe his mother and a strong suspicion that she was lying. "So where's he from, this man? What music hall?"

"Well..." His mother considered what might be the most credible answer. "I promised him faithfully that I wouldn't tell you, dearest. He wants to see you as you always are ... but if I give you a teeny weeny clue that he comes from somewhere beginning with 'Y' and ending in 'K', you might be able to guess."

"York!" Baby thought for a moment. York was quite near; his mother could be telling the truth. "All right – but I want to meet him afterwards."

"But then he'd know I'd been a naughty girl and told my boysie-woysie he was coming, and he'd be cross. We don't want to make him cross, do we?"

"I suppose." Baby shrugged. "All right..." He brightened as an idea came to him. "Get him on stage to check the padlocks on the chains! Then I can have a look at him."

"That might be difficult, dearest." Mrs Snicket made a mental note to pick some re-spectable-looking gentleman who might pass as a theatre impresario, and smiled at her son. "Now, shall we make sure everything's exactly how you want it?"

Things were not exactly as wanted over at The Golden Lion. The landlord was unmoved when Aunt Mags described the deeply unpleasant condition of the company's costumes and curtains; he shrugged, and suggested that the actions of his customers had nothing to do with him.

Sukie was more sympathetic. She promised to make sure the shed was securely bolted and barred, and remarked that it had been an unusually rowdy evening. "Didn't do my flower pots any good, neither. Happens, though ... them lads and lasses, they do like their ale, and they do like to sing their songs."

Pa brightened. "'Music has charms to soothe—'" he began.

"No, Fred." Aunt Mags glared at him.

Pa subsided and picked up one end of the offending hamper, Aunt Mags took the other end, and Charlie and Rosie walked behind with Gertie and Vinnie, as their little procession made its way onto the high street.

It was market day, and the road was crowded with men, women and children. Pa dropped the hamper and clapped his hands. "My dears! We must sing as we go: a rousing sea shanty, perhaps, or perchance a jolly round. We will enchant our future audience! We will—"

"No, we won't." Aunt Mags was red in the face and sweating. "There'll be no singing, Fred. These costumes smell appalling, and the sooner we get them to Uncaster Hall the better."

"They've got a huge washtub," Charlie said. "Edie showed us. It's big enough for a fish pond! Aunt Mags, why don't Rosie and I go on ahead to heat the water?"

Aunt Mags put down her end of the hamper so she could wipe the sweat out of her eyes. "Good idea."

Charlie nodded, and he and Rosie ran off. Passing the Supper Rooms, they paused for a moment. "What do you think the baby's like?" Rosie asked.

"Told you: he'll be our age," Charlie said. "Or maybe even older."

Rosie sighed. "I'd have liked it to be a little baby. Still, we'll see him tonight..."

"Rosie – look! Over there!" Charlie's tone was urgent, and Rosie swivelled round; when she saw Jago sweeping the steps she grabbed her brother's arm. "Charlie! It's that horrible boy! Don't let him see us!"

She was too late. Jago had already spotted them – he was scowling, and Rosie was convinced that he was about to dash at them when a shrill voice called his name. With a muttered oath, he turned and disappeared back inside; but not before shaking his fist.

"Will he be there tonight?" Rosie asked anxiously. "I don't like him. Not one little bit!"

"We'll all be together," Charlie told her. "If he tries to start anything, we'll set Aunt Mags on him!"

Rosie laughed, and she was smiling as they hurried back to the Hall.

They found Edie and Arabella in the kitchen: Arabella was trying to make a shopping list, and Edie was having a hard time keeping her Lady's ideas in check.

Arabella Poskett was used to passing her cook instructions; once these were given, luncheon, tea and dinner appeared as requested. Now she was faced with the realities of feeding eight people on six shillings a week – less, if possible, as the pile of bills was not getting any smaller – and her suggestions of duck, or capons, or a box of fresh white fish, were met with firm resistance.

"Honestly, Ma'am ... you can fill a lot of hungry bellies without bothering with them fancy things!" Edie said. "Me and my Gran and the little ones, we lived on nothing much more than bread and weak beer for ever such a long time, and it never did me no harm."

Arabella looked with compassion at the waiflike figure beside her, but said nothing except: "Maybe I'd better leave it to you after all, Edie dear. I was only trying to help."

Edie beamed. "And you do help, Ma'am. Gived me lots of good ideas, you have! Now, if we fetches in some greens from the garden, and a few more potatoes, could you clean 'em? And I'll run up the road to the butcher's. You can make ever such tasty soup with bone stock, and bones cost nothing!"

Arabella Poskett, who had never so much as boiled an egg for herself, sank back in despair. "I don't think I'm any good at anything anymore. Nobody ever told me about bone stock."

Rosie smiled at Arabella. "It was a lovely dinner last night! And we can all help. But we've got lots and lots of horrid dirty clothes to wash, and the curtains ... so can we use the washtub?"

"The washtub?" Arabella looked blank, but Edie, sensing an emergency, jumped up.

"If you gives me a hand, Charlie—" she paused for a fraction of a second to enjoy that she was allowed to call him Charlie— "we can fill the big copper tub with water. There's loads of old wood in the washhouse." Then, wondering if she had gone too far, she turned to her employer. "That all right with you, Ma'am?"

"What? Oh ... yes. Of course!" Arabella nodded. "What happened, Rosie?"

"It's the costumes," Rosie explained. "Someone opened the hamper and then he was sick."

"Puked all over everything," Charlie said cheerfully. "And it smells rank! And then he went to sleep on top of it, and if you ask me he wasn't just sick—"

"*Sh!*" Rosie hushed Charlie before he could shock their landlady with too much detail. "We can't use the curtains either. That's the worst. We could swap the costumes round – Aunt Mags thinks the ones at the bottom of the basket might be just about all right – but we have to have curtains."

"So we won't be opening the show until the end of the week," Charlie chimed in. "But we'll do lots of advertising, so hopefully everyone'll want to come. They'll be tired of Little Baby Bubbles by then, with any luck."

Edie was hovering in the doorway. "You coming, Charlie? That copper ain't going to fill itself, you know."

Charlie grinned. "Coming," he said, and he followed Edie out. Rosie looked at Arabella, who was still sitting at the table. She was gazing after Charlie and Edie with a wistful expression; Rosie, who was missing her mother, wondered if she was missing her children.

"I could help you with the vegetables, if you like," she offered, and Arabella gave her a grateful smile. She had, in fact, been wishing that Hypatia and Affogato were as sensible and practical as Charlie, Edie and Rosie.

With a sigh, Arabella pulled herself to her feet. "Thank you, Rosie dear. That would be very helpful indeed."

Fifteen

FOR THE REST OF THE DAY, STEAM ROSE steadily from the washhouse in Uncaster Hall as Aunt Mags and Gertie – purple and perspiring – battled with the weight of the sodden curtains and costumes.

Pa settled himself in the chilly drawing room to compose new songs for his version of *King Lear*, while Charlie helped Vinnie restring a banjo. Rosie, having discovered that Arabella was under the impression that potatoes grew on bushes and cabbages on trees, had made herself useful: a heap of washed vegetables was piled on the kitchen draining board. Arabella, exhausted by her lack of knowledge and general feelings of uselessness, had retired for a nap.

Once the chores were out of the way, Rosie and her new friend Edie set out together to visit the butcher's shop. They were so deep in conversation that they didn't notice a tall thin man striding towards them until he all but fell over them. As he recovered himself he dropped his leather case; Rosie picked it up for him, but instead of thanking her he snatched it away with a sharp exclamation of annoyance before striding off.

"What a horrible man!" Rosie said.

Edie nodded. "He nearly knocked me over yesterday."

Rosie glanced over her shoulder at the departing figure. "Wonder where he's off to in such a hurry?"

Arabella Poskett was woken from her nap by loud knocking at the front door. Aware that Edie was out, she put on her apron and went to see who it was, hoping against hope that it wasn't the bailiffs.

When she saw it was Olio Sleevery she was relieved, while wondering at the same time why he had bothered to call. He had never been a friend: she had heard too much about his reputation as a harsh and unforgiving landlord and, as he neither hunted, gambled nor drank to excess, the Honourable Henry had considered him unworthy of notice.

"As you see, Mr Sleevery, my circumstances are sadly changed," Arabella said. "I can offer little by way of refreshment after your journey…"

Olio Sleevery shook his head. "Only here to make you an offer," he said baldly. "Heard you're left with nothing but debts. Been talking to the shopkeepers. Bailiffs been here already." Arabella took a step back; Olio stepped forward. "They'll be back. Won't leave you alone. Take all you've got. Now, I can make you an offer. This place? Crumbling. Worth nothing. But I'll take it off your hands for five hundred pounds, contents included. That'll pay your debts, and leave you enough for a cottage. Nice little cottage: just the thing for a widow-woman."

"No, Mr Sleevery." Arabella was shocked by his directness. "I have no intention of leaving Uncaster Hall. My son will inherit it when he comes of age, just as his father did before him.

I have nothing more to say." She tried to close the door, but Olio Sleevery's foot was in the way.

"No more than I expected," he said. "You'll change your tune soon enough when the bailiffs are carting away your furniture. But I'll keep offering. Only thing is, the offer goes down. Next time it'll be four hundred and fifty. Remember that!"

He removed his foot, turned on his heel and marched away, leaving Arabella staring indignantly after him.

When Edie and Rosie got back carrying a heavy bag of bones, Arabella was wandering round the kitchen garden. She looked so lost that Rosie ran to her side.

"Are you missing your children?" she asked. "I'm so sorry. I miss my mother lots and lots, and my little brothers and sister too." She found she was blinking back tears, and wiped her eyes with the edge of her shawl.

Arabella, surprised but pleased by this sympathy, smiled at Rosie and patted her head. She had not, in fact, been thinking about Hypatia and Affogato; she had been thinking about her debts and Olio Sleevery's offer, and wondering if she had been foolish to dismiss him so high-handedly. Edie had given her a shilling from the six that the Steam Whistle Theatre Company had paid in rent, but it was all too obvious that one shilling a week was not going to solve her problems.

"Isn't your mother going to join you, dear?" she asked.

Rosie shook her head. "We've got to be a success first. Ma can't come unless we can send her the money for her ticket. We only just managed to pay for our own, you see ... and we didn't know what it would be like in the North. My little brother gets a bad chest ever so easily: we thought there might be snow and ice, and that would make him poorly."

Edie giggled. "Snow, Rosie? This ain't the North Pole!"

"I know that now," Rosie said. "And Billy would be better here. There's no smoke, and no fog ... it's the fog that makes him cough."

"My little sisters coughed ever so much, all day and all night." Edie, for the first time since

Rosie had met her, stopped smiling. "They never got enough to eat once they put us in the workhouse, and as for the damp – why, you never saw anything like it! Them rooms where they kept the little ones was running with water some days."

Rosie gazed at Edie, wide-eyed. "Where are they now?"

"Dead, Miss – I mean, Rosie." Edie turned her back, and blew her nose on a rag from her pocket.

Rosie, horrified, hurried towards her, but Arabella was there first. "Poor, poor little girls," she said, and folded Edie in her arms.

Edie stayed still for a long moment with her eyes tightly shut, then sniffed, smiled, and wriggled out of Arabella's embrace. "No need to be sorry for me, Ma'am," she said, "thanking you all the same. And there's things we ought to be doing right now. We got bone broth to make! Got the biggest bones you ever did see... Think he liked Rosie's pretty face. I'll get started right now." And she scuttled into the kitchen, clutching the bag of bones to her chest.

"Rosie dear, I'm sure I've already forgotten

which vegetable is which." Arabella, thinking Edie might like a moment to herself, waved a hand at the rows of carrots and cabbages.

Rosie began at once to point out the differences between beetroot and onions, but was interrupted by Charlie: "Pa wants you. He says you ought to start learning the new piece he's written – he's in the drawing room."

Rosie opened her mouth to argue, but Arabella gave her a gentle push. "You can show me another time, dear."

"I'd love to," Rosie said ... and she meant it.

A moment later she was skipping down the corridor to the drawing room, where the Steam Whistle Theatre Company's very own King Lear was standing by the mantelpiece, practising his lines.

"Daughter!" Pa flung out his arms. "Come hither and stand by me, thy loving father!"

Ignoring the invitation, Rosie asked, "Have you got a new piece for me?"

Pa handed her a scrawled piece of paper. "Here, Cordelia my pet – and your father has surpassed himself. There'll not be a dry eye in the house."

Rosie settled down to read it. A moment later, she looked up. "I like it, Pa!"

"Of course you do." Pa beamed at her. "And I had an idea worthy of William himself. Rosie, my darling – you're going to *sing* the last words of Cordelia!"

"Sing?" Rosie considered the idea. "But we haven't got a tune for it."

Pa put his finger to his lips, and beckoned Rosie nearer before pointing at the dusty grand piano in the corner of the room. "I've been peeking and peering, Rosie my angel. There's music on the stand! Songs! Delightful songs, written in that same looping hand that led us safely here – which leads me to suppose that our esteemed landlady, the gracious Mrs Poskett, is a pianist. Tonight I shall beg her to do us the honour of joining our little company ... and we will make the sweetest of music!"

"Tonight? Aren't we going to go and see the baby magician tonight, Pa?" Rosie asked.

Pa sighed, abandoned his dramatic pose, and put his arm round her. "I'm really sorry, pet. There's no money for tickets: I wish there was, but there isn't. As soon as we're back in funds I'll take you."

Rosie picked up her script and went to curl up in a corner. *Things must be really bad*, she thought, *if Pa's talking like that.*

She looked again at her new song. Once, long before, Ma had taken her and Charlie to a music hall to see Little Jolie Johnson, and when Little Jolie took her bow the audience had thrown pennies and threepenny bits and even sixpences and shillings onto the stage to show their appreciation. What if she could be as popular? The Steam Whistle Theatre Company would be rich, and Ma and the little ones could all come to Uncaster Hall...

Dreaming dreams of wealth and fame, Rosie fell asleep.

Sixteen

ELIZA SNICKET HAD KEPT BABY HAPPY WITH promises of future fame, several slices of pie and a large dish of chocolate. As the men began to fill the front benches of the Supper Rooms, she watched from behind the curtains of the shallow stage to see what kind of audience it would be.

An elderly man with a shining bald head was sitting at the upright piano, playing tunes that Mrs Snicket recognized as having been all the rage in London several years before.

Old fashioned. Likely to be respectable, then, she told herself.

Baby was sitting on a box picking his nose, while Mrs Moore spoke in angry whispers to a flushed and damp-haired Canary of Covent Garden.

"We've usually begun our entertainment by now," she said, and her nose was very sharp. "I asked you to be here at seven-thirty, Miss Gracegirdle. I trust you'll do better tomorrow!"

Gertie had only remembered her date at the Supper Rooms as she and Aunt Mags were pegging out the heavy curtains on the washing line, and had had to run all the way from Uncaster Hall.

"Of course." She tried not to look as out of breath as she felt, and surreptitiously adjusted her corset which, if too tight, restricted her high notes. "May I give my music to your pianist?"

Mrs Moore raised her eyebrows. "Don't you accompany yourself?"

"I prefer not to," Gertie said. Her piano playing was restricted to picking out the semblance of a tune with one finger – but that was none of Mrs Moore's business. "In Covent Garden, it was considered infinitely more professional to have an accompanist."

"Is that so?" Mrs Moore refused to be impressed. "Give me the music, and I'll pass it to

Gordon. Now, are you ready? We're already clearing the soup bowls. I want Little Baby Bubbles to begin before we serve the entrées, so you've only got as long as it takes for the oysters and the fish to be served and eaten." She disappeared through the curtains, and there was an expectant lull in the babble of conversation. Slipping back again, she nodded at Gertie. "You're on."

Gertie opened her mouth to ask where her introduction was going to come from, but changed her mind when she saw Mrs Moore's frosty expression. A twirl of notes from the piano sent her hurrying forward; taking a deep breath she burst into song.

Baby finished exploring the contents of his nose and listened. He had considered making a fuss and refusing to perform if Gertie made any future appearances, but her first words caught his attention and his frown faded...

The boy is so magical, magical, magical,
Nothing in life is quite what it seems.
This is the boy I have longed for forever,
This is the boy who makes real my dreams!

Gertie warbled on. As she finished there was a mere spatter of applause; the audience were attacking their fish, and although there were smiles and nods and approving murmurs, it was hard to clap with a knife in one hand and fork in the other.

The Maestro of Magic, behind the curtain and unaware of these restrictions, was reassured by what he heard. Any show of enthusiasm would have been troubling: he was the main attraction, and the audience needed to know that. He straightened his star-spangled cloak and stood up as Gertie came back.

"Pleasant enough," she said as she passed him. "Noisy eaters, though. Clattering their cutlery as if they haven't eaten for a week... And there's a dreadful smell of fish!"

Mrs Moore, who was waiting to introduce Baby, glared at her. "I'll see you tomorrow. And make sure you're on time, Miss Gracegirdle!" Gertie rolled her eyes, and slipped away to watch.

"And now, Ladies and Gentlemen, the event you've all been waiting for!" Mrs Moore clapped her hands to make sure her diners were paying attention. "Straight from an enormously successful season in the great metropolis – and now here, in our very own Uncaster. I ask you to give a wonderful welcome to Little Baby Bubbles, the one and only child escapologist and master of magic ... and only eight years old!"

The curtains opened to deafening cheers and Baby stepped forward. His costume was carefully designed by his mother to make him look as young as possible, and he had learned to slouch to disguise his height. Even so he bore little resemblance to an eight-year-old, sporting as he did the suspicion of a moustache. If he noticed the sudden, surprised hush that followed his appearance he showed no sign of it, and he ignored the small girl at the back of the room who shouted, "Where's the baby?" Buoyed up by Gertie's song he swept off his silver top hat before there could be any further comment – and there was a universal gasp of astonishment as a large bunch of flowers sprang up inside.

Uncaster had seen few magicians, and as Baby went through his routine he was rewarded with enthusiastic shouts of, "Do it again, laddie! Do it again!" Even the noise of endless plates being scraped clean, and the rattling and clashing of cutlery, didn't upset him as much as it usually would have; the wild thumping of beer mugs after a particularly cunning piece of sleight of hand made up for it.

Jago, frozen to the spot in wonder, had to be prodded in the back before he got on with handing round thick slices of well-boiled beef. The other serving boys were equally fascinated: gravy was spilt, sauces forgotten and spoons dropped – but nobody complained.

The room grew hotter and hotter as the meal and the show went on. The smell of overcooked meat and vegetables thickened, the floor grew sticky with spilled beer, and the shouting and exclamations of amazement grew louder and louder. When Eliza Snicket wound Baby round and round in chains, aided by an overawed and sweaty young greengrocer, the crowd were so excited that Mrs Moore, watching from the back of the stage, began to feel anxious.

Fortunately Baby burst his bonds quickly. As he took his final bow the cheering and stamping reached a deafening crescendo – before fading away as dishes of orange water ice, designed to cool passions as well as palates, were passed round.

Baby bowed a second time, and left the stage in triumph.

"Darling dearest boy!" His mother rushed to embrace her son as the curtains closed behind him, but Baby ducked out of the way.

"When do we meet the man from York?" he demanded.

Mrs Snicket, who had been mentally counting up shillings and sixpences (and coming to many pleasant conclusions), blinked at this sudden attack.

Baby came closer and stared at her, his piggy little eyes as sharp as gimlets. "You said he'd be here! Where is he?" And then, when his mother didn't answer, he pushed his face into hers, breathing hard. "He'd better be here! Tell me he's here – or I'll never, ever, EVER do another show again!"

"My darling precious, didn't you see him?" Mrs Snicket pulled herself together. "He never took his eyes off you! He was enchanted! Absolutely enchanted! But it's like I told you, he had to dash away the moment you finished to catch his train to York. You'll be hearing from him very, very soon."

"You never said he had to catch a train!" Baby was almost sure that his mother was lying, but his urgent desire to be appreciated made him unusually susceptible to her wiles. "Where was he sitting?"

Eliza Snicket tapped the side of her nose. "You needed sharp eyes, my darling. He was lurking by that pillar at the back of the room. He didn't want you to see him!"

Baby gave in – more because he wanted to believe her than because he did. "He'd better write soon. Someone might come from London and see how brilliant I am, and snatch me away!"

"Indeed they might," Mrs Snicket agreed. "But now come and lie down, my clever, clever boy. You deserve a rest."

As Baby was led away by his mother, Gertie was walking back to Uncaster Hall. Music halls, theatres and supper-room entertainments were what she knew best, and she recognized

Baby's performance as proficient – but nothing out of the ordinary. The reaction of the Uncaster audience had intrigued her; a London crowd would have been restless at best, and at worst downright rude.

Small town folk, she told herself. *They've obviously not seen much in the way of shows. But if they think second-class magic is something special, what'll they make of* King Lear?

Reaching the kitchen, she was surprised to find it empty – but the sound of crashing and banging sent her to the drawing room. Opening the door, she found a rehearsal in progress: Pa was sitting on the floor, walloping a saucepan with a wooden spoon, and Rosie was kneeling beside him. Aunt Mags and Arabella Poskett were sitting side by side at the piano frowning at sheets of music, while Vinnie, banjo in hand, was talking to Charlie and Edie.

They all stopped what they were doing as Gertie came in and looked at her expectantly.

"So?" Rosie asked eagerly. "What was he like? Was he very clever?"

Gertie shook her head. "He's just an overgrown schoolboy who can do a few tricks."

Pa got up, looking delighted. "So the Steam Whistle Theatre Company will win all hearts and minds!"

Gertie shook her head again. "I don't know, Fred... The audience loved it! Cheering, stamping – they couldn't get enough of him! I don't think they'd ever seen anything like it before."

"Probably hadn't." Vinnie said gloomily. "Small place like this. Won't get any of the decent touring shows, not with York so close by – can't think why they've even got a station, come to that." He gave Pa a reproachful look. "We'd have done better in York, you know."

Pa picked up his saucepan and gave it a whack with his spoon. "Couldn't afford the tickets, Vinnie. But after our triumphant season here, the world will be ours for the taking ... so rise up, my souls! Let vaulting ambition carry us ever onward: throw your hearts over the windmill, sing to the sun, and all will be well."

Aunt Mags turned her back on Pa and gave Gertie a searching look. "So you don't think *King Lear* is right for Uncaster?"

"I don't know." Gertie shrugged. "They liked my song, and that's a silly, sentimental little piece. I'd say we'd maybe be best doing something simpler than Shakespeare – at least to start off with."

Pa was appalled. "No, no, no! We must shoot for the stars!"

"Mrs Poskett's found a lovely tune for my Cordelia song," Rosie said. "She says she used to play it when she was a little girl, and it fits the words beautifully. It'd be a shame to waste it..."

Vinnie put the banjo down. "What about *A Midsummer Night's Dream*? Still Shakespeare, but easier to understand."

"They wouldn't like that at all." Charlie, terrified of being told he had to play Puck, decided to support his father. "All those weavers and tailors ... they'd think we were laughing at them."

Vinnie nodded. "Good point. *The Tempest*?"

But Pa was not to be moved: he had decided on *King Lear*, and that was that. Gertie and Aunt Mags shook their heads at each other, but, knowing Pa as well as they did, they made no further efforts to dissuade him.

Arabella got off her piano stool and came

to join the company. "*King Lear* is quite a substantial play, isn't it?" she asked innocently. "I remember my governess telling me about a performance she saw in London. She said it was terribly long, but the actor who was Lear – I think his name was 'Macready'? – made it bearable. She didn't sleep longer than ten minutes the entire time!"

Pa – shocked to the core by the idea of anyone sleeping through *King Lear*, but delighted to be asked about his favourite subject – brightened. "It is indeed one of the longest plays, dear lady ... although *Hamlet* is longer. I've taken the liberty of making a few cuts and alterations, so we run for about an hour."

"Fifty-five minutes too long," Vinnie muttered, but only Edie heard him.

Puzzled by his comment, she tapped him on the arm. "What's it about, mister? Was he a real king? Is it funny?"

Vinnie sighed. "Funny? Not at all. It's about a king who has three daughters; two nasty ones and one who's much too truthful, and that upsets him. He ends up with nothing, goes mad and dies."

Edie's eyes opened very wide. "Oh." She thought for a moment. "Do you do that one for free?"

"Goodness me, no!" Vinnie scratched his head. "Why on Earth would we do it for free?"

"Well..." Edie was trying to think of a way to be tactful. "Seems to me as there's plenty of folks what ends up with nothing and goes mad. You should have seen old Granfer Hinson in the workhouse! He was madder than a wasp in a vinegar bottle, but nobody never paid nothing to look at him. Weren't a pretty sight, 'specially when he was dribbling."

Before Vinnie could answer, Pa stepped into the centre of the room and clapped his hands. "My dears! Let us rise early tomorrow: there is much to do, and we must be ready for our grand opening." He turned to Aunt Mags. "Our costumes and curtains – how long will it be before they are restored to us?"

"If you mean, 'When will they be dry?', I'd say not for another two days – and that's only if it doesn't rain." Aunt Mags' hands were red and raw from scrubbing and hot water, and she was sure Cordelia's gown had shrunk. She turned to Gertie. "We left you a bowl of chicken soup, Gertie, if you're hungry."

Edie jumped to her feet. "Shall I fetch it for you, Miss? Won't take me a minute to warm it through. And there's a couple of cold potatoes, if you'd like them."

Gertie smiled at her. "Thank you, Edie, but I can do it. You've been working all day."

"And so have you! And doing singing as well as all that washing... No – leave it to me, Miss."

"I'll help you, Edie," Charlie said, and Rosie looked at him in surprise. He was not usually enthusiastic about domestic duties, but he was already out of his seat and heading for the door.

Vinnie saw Rosie's expression, and grinned. "She's a pretty girl, Rosie."

Rosie giggled. "A horrible boy at the Supper Rooms said Charlie was Edie's 'beau'."

"He could do a lot worse," Vinnie said. "She's got a big heart."

Aunt Mags, hearing Rosie's voice, swung round. "Rosie! Are you still here? Off to bed, young lady! It's late, and as far as I'm aware Cordelia didn't have big black shadows under her eyes... Not at the beginning of the play, anyway!"

"All right." Rosie yawned. "Tell Charlie to bring up a candle. I'll see you in the morning."

Pa held out his arms. "Sleep well, pet." He kissed the top of her head. "Sweet dreams!"

Seventeen

THE NEXT DAY STARTED BADLY FOR THE Steam Whistle Theatre Company: they woke to find driving rain lashing the windows, and when Edie went to collect the eggs she discovered a fox had got into the hen run and carried off Brown Betty. The remaining chickens were in such a state of anxiety none of them had laid. Breakfast was a bleak affair.

Arabella was depressed by more than the weather. The morning's post had brought her a brief note from Aunt Jocasta – written in a firm and upright hand, it stated that Affogato and Hypatia had arrived, and had been accommodated. There was no mention of their return, and no word from either of the children: Arabella sighed, and took her tea to her boudoir.

Edie, going to clear away the breakfast plates, found Charlie, Rosie, Aunt Mags and Gertie staring gloomily at the heavily laden washing lines, drooping in the garden.

"That'll never dry out there," she said. "Not in this weather. It ain't raining cats and dogs, it's raining camelphants and hippobottomuses. We could string up a line in the stables; there ain't no horses there no more, and it's dry."

This idea provided strenuous occupation for the next couple of hours, and by late morning both the weather and the company's spirits had lifted a little.

"That'll please Pa," Rosie said. "He's gone to tell The Golden Lion we can't open there just yet. He'll be ever so pleased there's a chance of getting everything dry by the weekend..."

Pa had *not* been cheered by his visit to the Lion. The landlord had shown little interest in his news; Sukie had remarked that it was a shame – but had he heard there was a child magician at the Supper Rooms, and everyone was going to see him?

"I might have noticed a poster or two," Pa

lied. "The charm of a child! Of course, the Steam Whistle Theatre Company has not one but *two* delightful children."

"Do they do magic?" Sukie asked. "George says once your theatre's been and gone, we'll be looking for a magic act. Brings in the punters better than anything, he says."

Pa left the Lion under a cloud; a cloud that was darkened by the sight of a queue waiting outside the Supper Rooms. As he passed, Jago appeared on the doorstep, carrying a sign announcing that the evening's performance was sold out and no more tickets would be available until the next day. He pasted it up with a flourish, and made a face at the small boy nearest the door.

"Yah!" he said. "You're too late!" The small boy burst into tears; the queue muttered, and began to disperse.

Pa hurried towards them, hands outstretched. "Ladies, gentlemen, girls and boys! May I have your attention! The Steam Whistle Theatre Company will soon be performing at The Golden Lion … don't miss the chance to see us present *King Lear*. A once in a lifetime opportunity: seize it while you can!"

"Oi!" Standing in the doorway of the Supper Rooms, Jago was glaring at Pa. "You, old man! Get away! We don't want none of that kind of chat here. Don't you try riding on our coat tails – go and get an audience of your own, if you can. Stupid little company like yours ... shoo! *Shoo!*" And he picked up his paste brush and lunged at Pa.

Pa, realising the crowd was relishing the confrontation, made a hurried exit.

Jago saw him on his way with a sneer, and went to report the incident to Mrs Moore and Mrs Snicket; the report made much of his own wit and bravery, and painted Pa as an outrageous chancer. Both women were delighted; Jago was praised to the skies, and rewarded with a large slice of bread and jam. He was not as grateful as he might have been; he had seen the heaped up coins on Mrs Moore's office table, and was expecting sixpence at the very least.

Mrs Snicket was also interested in the shillings, sixpences, threepenny pieces and assorted coppers. "Do let me help you count our takings, dear Mrs Moore! Such a very satisfactory night, last night ... and sold out again tonight! Although I'm not at all surprised: my darling Baby is the master of his art. And you must let me take it to the bank for you, I'm sure your domestic duties are always very pressing."

Mrs Moore, who never let anyone into her inner sanctum, was taken aback by this offer. It would be beyond foolish to upset the mother of such a Golden Goose, however, so she agreed with a reasonable appearance of amicability. By the end of an hour they had agreed a total, and Mrs Snicket had retired to take Baby a cold collation of ham and chicken in order to keep his strength up.

She left Mrs Moore marvelling at how clumsy the child magician's mother had suddenly become; twice she had knocked the table so hard that coins had tumbled all over the floor. She had had to kneel to pick them up, loudly lamenting her foolishness. Mrs Moore, carefully counting her share of the money into a cloth bag, was inclined to believe she had rather less than half of the takings – and she grew thoughtful.

Was there something a little slippery about Eliza Snicket?

Tying the bag with a couple of firm knots, she decided it would harm no one if she kept a watchful eye on her lodger.

The rain had eased to a mere drizzle as Pa stomped back to Uncaster Hall, brooding darkly on Jago's behaviour.

"Rude. That's what it was! Rude! It's a free country."

A sense of injustice became mixed with increasing anxiety about the future, and he was so deep in thought that he was unaware of Rosie and Charlie's approach.

"Pa? What's the matter? We've been waving for ages and you didn't see us!"

Pa pulled himself together. "My precious darlings! No, no. All is well. And where are you off to, looking so bonny and blithe?"

Rosie wasn't fooled by her father's cheerfulness. "Pa, you're worrying. Is it the curtains? Only, Edie had a wonderful idea and we've hung everything in the stables. Aunt Mags thinks they'll be ready to use on Saturday!"

"Saturday?" Pa's smile was enormous. "Then all is not lost! We must throw our hearts into our endeavours." He spun round in a circle, hands on hips. "Flyers! We must have advertising flyers, thousands of them ... and posters! We have to make certain that every man, woman and child in Uncaster knows that – at last! – the Steam Whistle Theatre Company is ready to show them the glories of Shakespeare. I must hurry away to shake the last coins from our money bags and set all in motion. Farewell, my dears!"

Rosie looked at Charlie. Gertie had mentioned the subject of flyers, and Aunt Mags had been crushing in her reply: "No money, Gertie. Not a penny. If we don't get some kind of show up and running very soon we're lost. There's no money left for flyers, or any kind of extras. We can't even go back to London because we can't afford the tickets. I don't know what we'll do – I'm trying not to think about it."

The children had listened, but said nothing. Once they had been released from laundry duty in the stables, their arms aching and their hands wrinkled like prunes, they had hurried into a corner.

Rosie was terrified at the idea of not being able to get back to London and Ma; Charlie, meanwhile, was worried about the future of the company. But they were united in their belief that something had to be done: if the adults weren't going to take any action, then the children would. They had come up with a plan, a daring plan that they were on their way to putting into action.

They watched as their father strode down the road, oblivious to the misting rain and the puddles, before turning to head up the high street. Rosie made sure they were on the other side of the road from the Supper Rooms; she had no wish to see or hear Jago.

Once they were outside The Golden Lion, Rosie stopped. "You don't think we should have checked with Aunt Mags about this, do you?" she asked.

Charlie shook his head. "She'd have said no. But just think of her face when we come back this evening with loads of money! Pa can have his flyers and posters, and we can pay the rent for next week!" He shoved his hands in his pockets and leant back against the wall in a lordly pose. "I might even buy you and Edie ribbons from that shop you're always going on about."

"I'll buy them for myself," Rosie told him. "It'll be both of us earning it. But you can buy some for Edie if you want." She gave Charlie a sideways look and was almost sure he was blushing. "You like her, don't you?"

"So we'd better go and ask," Charlie said, ignoring her. "Are you ready?"

Rosie shook out her damp shawl and folded it neatly round her shoulders. "Ready."

Eighteen

IN THE SUPPER ROOMS, LITTLE BABY BUBBLES was celebrating the success of the previous evening by spending the day lying on the chaise longue in Mrs Moore's private parlour, demanding food and drink at regular intervals.

Mrs Moore, in between chivvying her cook and issuing orders to her kitchen staff in preparation for another busy evening, was doing her best to smile and provide the little delicacies he ordered. Fortunately Jago, fascinated by Baby's skill with coins and cards, was unusually willing to fetch and carry.

Little did Mrs Moore know he was considering leaving the Supper Rooms and striking out on his own – and had decided the best way was to persuade Baby to hand over his secrets...

Mrs Snicket hung over Baby as if he really were a fragile infant, cooing and whispering to him. When there was a loud and authoritative knocking on the front door, her only thought was that it might disturb Baby – who had dozed off, his mouth wide open. But when Baby continued to snore, she was reassured and took no further notice of the voices outside.

It was only the repetition of the word "thief" that caught her attention; leaving Baby to his slumbers she crept to the door to listen more carefully.

"This, Constable Grimshaw, is a most respectable establishment!" Mrs Moore was clearly outraged. "There has never, in all my time here, been any theft or larceny of any kind!"

"That bain't any proof it didn't happen last night, Missus." Constable Grimshaw was firm. "A young gentleman's reported his pocketbook taken, a pocketbook containing ten one pound notes."

"I expect he mislaid it." Mrs Moore was unmoved. "Many's the man who's left a pocketbook lying around."

Constable Grimshaw coughed. "You might be

right there, Missus, but the gentleman's wife can vouch for him having it with him as he entered your rooms. *And* he noticed the loss as he was leaving. QEDeedle, as you might say." The constable was evidently pleased with this pronouncement, as he repeated it: "That's what the law says, if you care to look. QEDeedle."

Mrs Snicket's hand stole to her pocket and rested there.

Mrs Moore, disconcerted not by the constable's grasp of legal Latin, but by the details of the theft, tried again. "It might well have fallen to the floor under a table. I'll ask one of my staff to run and look—"

"No, Missus. If you've no objections – and 'tis my right by law – I'll have a look myself." Then, in a more conciliatory tone, Constable Grimshaw added: "He'll not get far, whoever he is. All the notes were new printed, so the bank's got the numbers writ safely down. Fortunate, you might say."

Mrs Snicket did not wait to hear Mrs Moore's reply. She stepped out of the parlour, and greeted the policeman with a cry of surprise. "A policeman! My goodness! Are we all to be arrested, Mrs Moore?" And she gave a merry girlish laugh.

Constable Grimshaw inspected her with interest. "Would you be the mother of the child magician, Ma'am?"

"Indeed I am." Mrs Snicket fluttered a little. "And I do hope you'll come and see my Baby perform very, very soon. A wonder! Cheered to the rafters last night."

"The gentleman that I'm here on behalf of, he told me he was of use to you during the performance. Tied the young man up, he says."

"Oh!" Mrs Snicket trilled another merry laugh. "That dear man! I hope he's not in any trouble?"

"Lost his pocketbook, Ma'am. Terrible... I don't suppose as you noticed anything, whilst he was aiding and abetting you in the tying up of the child magician?"

Baby's mother put her finger on her lip in an enchantingly childlike manner, while she thought about this tricky question. "Did I notice anything? I think not. The audience were cheering so loudly, I wouldn't have heard anything fall."

Mrs Moore, who had enjoyed the anticipatory hush as Little Baby Bubbles was loaded with chains, raised her eyebrows – but said nothing.

"That poor man … how worried he must be. Ten pounds – a remarkable sum, although perhaps just a little unwise to carry so much upon his person." Mrs Snicket spun round and headed for the door that led to the supper room. "But we must search! We must search high and low." Before the constable could say a word to stop her, she had gone.

"Well, well, well. A most enthusiastic lady," Constable Grimshaw observed.

"*Most* enthusiastic." That Mrs Snicket had known the pocketbook contained ten pounds had not gone unnoticed by Mrs Moore. She sounded dry as she added, "Hadn't you better go about your search?"

But before the constable and Mrs Moore had reached the door of the supper room, they met a jubilant Mrs Snicket coming towards them – holding a leather pocketbook. "Under the chains!" she announced. "A little dusty, but I hope unscathed. Do check, Mr Inspector: make sure the money is there!"

Constable Grimshaw took the pocketbook. Opening it, he carefully counted out the notes; once he had arrived at ten he nodded. "The gentleman will be much relieved," he said. "And I thank you, Ma'am, for your help." He turned to Mrs Moore. "You too, Missus. And now, if you'll excuse me, I'll be on my way to return the property to its owner."

"Do come and see our show!" Mrs Snicket's smile was dazzling. "Of course, we're completely sold out tonight ... but I'm sure our dearest Mrs Moore could accommodate you. And your lady wife as well, should she wish to come."

"A kind offer. I'll ask my old lady!" Constable Grimshaw bowed, and stomped away.

Mrs Moore was suffering from an internal battle. She was increasingly certain that her companion was a thief – but Mrs Snicket was also the mother of the child magician. Any accusation would immediately cut off what promised to be a substantial income for some time to come; an income that was very welcome.

Perhaps a subtle warning would be enough?

"A most unfortunate occurrence." She gave

Mrs Snicket a hard stare. "Let us hope nothing like that *ever* happens again. We have an excellent reputation here, and I would be seriously disappointed should that reputation be sullied."

Mrs Snicket put a soothing hand on Mrs Moore's arm. "Oh, how I agree. It was your wonderful reputation that brought me and my darling Baby to Uncaster! Believe you me, my dear, I have your interests as close to my heart as my own. But now I must run and see if Baby is in need of anything..." She fluttered away, leaving Mrs Moore considering what was best to do.

I shall buy a safe for the takings, Mrs Moore decided. *An iron safe, with a padlock... And I – and only I! – will have the key.*

Nineteen

ROSIE'S HEART WAS BEATING FAST AS SHE AND Charlie walked into The Golden Lion. The gloomy George was at his usual occupation of polishing the glasses and the pewter mugs, while Sukie was serving the regulars who arrived early and only left when she heaved them bodily out into the street. They took no notice of the children.

"Excuse me..." Charlie decided Sukie was likely to be more approachable. "Rosie and me, we're part of the Steam Whistle Theatre Company."

George looked up from his mugs. "If you're after your Pa, he's been and gone. You're too late." He gave a dismissive snort. "Said you'd not be performing for a while... Knew you was a shaky lot."

"No..." Charlie had practised his speech on the way but now he was finding it difficult to remember the words. "We're not looking for Pa, we're here to make you an offer. Rosie and me – we can sing. We can sing to your customers tonight, and every night until we've got our play on the stage."

"Sing?" George looked doubtful, but Sukie put down her pitcher of beer and smiled.

"Could be an idea. But what's in it for you, pet?"

Charlie smiled back at her. "We'd like to take a hat round at the end."

"Always after something," George growled. "Should do as you promised: plays is plays, and singing is singing. If you could do magic, mind, that'd be another story altogether... But your Pa says you can't, so you ain't no good to me."

"Give 'em a chance, George!" Sukie folded her arms. "Why shouldn't they make a copper or two? Tell you what, my pets, you come here tonight and we'll see how it goes. You'll need to be finished by nine, though – gets a bit rough after then... But the earlies, they might like a song or two. 'Specially if they can have a bit of a singsong themselves."

"Thank you!" Charlie's thanks were heart-felt, and Rosie curtsied.

Sukie, much amused, picked up her pitcher. "Now be off with you, you and your fancy curtsies! Some of us has work to do!"

As soon as they were outside, Rosie rushed at Charlie and hugged him. "We did it!"

"I did it, you mean," Charlie said. "You never said a word!"

"I curtsied." Rosie was indignant.

"As if that made any difference." Charlie made a face at her. "You'll have to sing extra songs to make up for it."

Rosie took no notice. "Will we tell Pa and Aunt Mags now?"

"No." Charlie shook his head. "Let's wait until tonight – we can walk in and pour the coppers all over the kitchen table!"

"Oh YES! And they'll be so surprised!" Rosie's eyes were shining as she imagined the scene. "We'll be the saviours of the company."

"We'll say we're going to walk to the Supper Rooms with Gertie," Charlie said. "And then we'll go on from there. It'll work out wonderfully, because we'll be coming back about the same time as she finishes! Nobody'll suspect a thing."

At Uncaster Hall, Edie, Aunt Mags and Gertie were busy making a beef and vegetable stew – with a great many vegetables, and very little beef. Arabella, who had cut herself twice and muddled the salt and the sugar, had been sent away to sweep the corridor. Pa had decided to make himself useful in the garden, and he and Vinnie were weeding out dandelions with a pleasant sense that they were major contributors to the functioning of the Hall.

Only Arabella heard the knock on the front door. Opening it, broom in hand, she was not entirely surprised to see Olio Sleevery leering at her from under a large black umbrella.

"Changed your mind?" he asked. "Think about it! Four hundred and fifty pounds. All debts paid, and a cottage of your own. But tomorrow it'll be four hundred. And day after, three fifty, then three hundred – and that'll only just pay the debts." Seeing Arabella's look of astonishment, he added, "It's me you owe now, you see."

He patted his leather case.

"Been buying up your bills. Been at it all day. Knew you couldn't pay. Butcher, stables, milliner, tailor. All of them glad to be paid. But don't think you'll get any more credit. I've made sure of that." He gave a sly wink; a wink that made him look like a conspiratorial rat. "So be a sensible woman, and take the offer." He opened his case, and brought out a formal looking document. "One signature, and you're free."

Arabella clutched at the door handle. Her head was spinning. "Not now," she managed. "Go away! I ... I need time. I can't say anything now... I need time to consider."

She was so pale that Olio hesitated.

"Tell you what," he said. "I'll do you a favour. I'll stretch a point. I'll leave the offer at four hundred until the weekend. But after that, nothing! I'll have the bailiffs in next week if you're foolish enough to deny me. *My* bailiffs. Not that ramshackle lot who came before." He gave a disgusted grunt. "Promising you what they couldn't promise – it'll be the real thing next time. Do you understand? DO YOU UNDERSTAND?"

And he pushed his sharp pointed nose so close to Arabella's face that she could see the long black whiskers in his nostrils.

"Yes," she whispered. "Yes ... I understand."

"Good." As Arabella leant against the wall to catch her breath, Olio walked briskly away.

At the end of the drive he met Rosie and Charlie, and he was so certain that Arabella would agree to his demands that he sneered at them. "Think you've got delightful rooms to stay in, do you? Think again. This place is going to be mine. And when it is, there'll be no room for trash like you. The gates will be closed. Closed and locked! So enjoy your last few days here." And with a mirthless chuckle, he left them staring after him in astonishment.

"Charlie!" Rosie clutched her brother's arm. "What did he mean?"

"I don't know," Charlie said. "Come on ... let's ask Mrs Poskett."

They found Arabella sitting on the front step, her head in her hands. At first she didn't seem to notice them, but when Charlie cleared his throat she looked up. She had recovered a little, though was still very pale.

Rosie knelt down beside her. "Are you all right? We've just met a really horrible man, and he said Uncaster Hall's going to belong to him! It isn't, is it?"

Charlie sat down on her other side. "You mustn't let him bully you! People like that don't deserve to get their own way, they really don't."

Arabella heaved a massive sigh. "But it seems I owe him money. I owe him a *lot* of money, and I've no way of paying him."

"Isn't there anyone who could help you?" Rosie asked.

"I wish there were." Arabella sighed again.

"But what will your children think?" Charlie's parents had never owned a house, and he was trying to imagine how he'd feel if a wonderful place like Uncaster Hall were taken away from him. "Won't they be terribly upset?"

"I don't think they will, my dear." Arabella sounded even more despondent. "They've gone to live with their aunt – my husband's sister – and she's rich. Very, very rich ... and they'll be much happier there."

"She's rich?" Charlie brightened. "Then surely she can help?"

"I'm afraid she doesn't like me." Sitting on a cold stone step outside her husband's ancestral home, the Honourable Henry Poskett's widow had no pride left. "She was furious when Henry married me ... I'm not grand, you see. My father was a nobody before he made money from his factories. And she's as grand as grand can be; she's the Honourable Jocasta Poskett. She was brought up here, but she's never once been to visit – not even to see the children."

"I think you should write to her." Charlie sounded so certain that Arabella looked at him in astonishment. "Write and ask her for help. Even if she doesn't like you, surely she'll be angry if that man is living here instead of you?"

Charlie's enthusiasm was infectious, and the colour came back to Arabella's face. "It wouldn't hurt to try, would it? She can only say no."

"I'm sure she'll say yes." Rosie's cheeks were pink with excitement. "That's what happens in all the plays we do. The orphan thinks that nobody loves her and she's all alone in the world, but then she helps a rich old lady cross the road and she gets adopted. Oh, and it turns out that the old lady is actually the orphan's grandmother that she lost a long time ago, and they recognize each other because they've each got half a silver sixpence—"

"Nobody's got any silver sixpences," Charlie told her. "That's the whole trouble... If you write the letter now, Mrs Poskett, we can take it to the Post Office."

For the first time in days Arabella felt a faint stirring of hope. Was it possible that Aunt Jocasta might feel some kind of affection for Uncaster Hall? She hugged Rosie before declaring, "I don't think I've got a long lost grandmother, dearest girl, but I'll write the letter straight away – and thank you very much." She stood up. "And perhaps ... if you don't mind, that is ... we could keep this a secret between us and Edie? Just for now? I don't want your family worried unnecessarily."

"Of course," said Charlie.

Rosie smiled. "It'll be all right, Mrs Poskett – it always is in the plays!"

Twenty

THE STEAM WHISTLE THEATRE COMPANY sat down to their vegetable and beef stew at six o'clock that evening. Gertie was anxious not to be late arriving at the Supper Rooms and, as there had been little else to eat that day, everyone was happy to join her.

Aunt Mags, in particular, had been hoping a good meal would calm Pa down; there had been a furious exchange when he came bouncing back full of ideas to swamp Uncaster high street with advertising flyers and posters. Even when shown the few remaining coppers, he had refused to be convinced that Aunt Mags hadn't forgotten a private store of shillings – the discussion had ended with him storming off. Aunt Mags, grim of face, had picked up a meat cleaver and reduced a cabbage to shreds in order to relieve her feelings.

Arabella had managed, after several false starts, to write her letter to the Honourable Jocasta Poskett. Pleased to have been able to do something positive, she sealed the letter with a flourish and hurried downstairs – only to find Pa standing in the hallway staring at the wall with a thunderous expression.

"Mr Pringle! Is something wrong?"

Pa came out of his reverie with a jump. "No, no, dear lady..." And then, seeing how sympathetic Arabella looked, he added, "A mere passing trouble. A question of advertising, as you might say ... or rather, a failure to advertise. And a failure to advertise will mean minimal audiences, and *that* will have the most severe consequences."

Arabella was struggling to understand. "You need to advertise your play?"

"Indeed we do, but alas!" Pa slapped his forehead to express his intense frustration. "We have no flyers!"

A lengthy explanation followed, from which Arabella emerged with a somewhat clearer idea of the intricacies of putting on a theatrical performance.

"But Mr Pringle! If these flyers are beyond your means, could you not write them yourself? I have little I can offer you, but ink and paper I do have. My husband had an idea that he would record the pedigrees of all his horses, but he never began…"

The suggestion was irresistible and Pa accepted with enthusiasm. When Arabella offered to help write them he refused at first, thinking such a task beneath her – but she insisted, and his world was bathed in golden light once more.

By the time they sat down for dinner they had been busy for some time, and Aunt Mags' fears of a tempestuous meal proved groundless. When Charlie and Rosie mentioned that they were going to walk to the Supper Rooms with Gertie, it was Pa's suggestion that Edie go with them.

"Have fun tonight, my precious children, for tomorrow we will be hard at work!"

Edie was delighted at the thought of keeping Charlie and Rosie company, and rushed off to wash her face and hands at the pump in the yard. She came back looking pink-cheeked and damp-haired – and Charlie looked at her admiringly.

He stepped forward, and offered her his arm. "May I take you walking, Miss Edie? And you, Miss Rosie – might you care to join us?"

Rosie giggled, but Edie dropped a curtsey. "Charmed, I'm sure."

Gertie laughed. "Goodness!" She turned to Vinnie. "You could learn a lesson from Charlie, Vincent. How about you escort me to the Supper Rooms?"

Vinnie stood up and bowed. "Of course, my dear. Whatever you wish."

He began to leave the table, but Pa put a restraining hand on his arm. "Dear boy! We could do with your assistance here, if your good lady will forgive me. Two hundred flyers! Two hundred by tomorrow, that is my aim... And you have a fine hand at writing."

"It's all right, Vinnie." Gertie gave him a dismissive wave. "I'll walk with the children. We need those flyers."

◆　◆　◆

The sky had cleared by the time the three children followed Gertie out into the evening air, although the trees were still heavy with rain.

Gertie shivered as a low branch showered her with drops, and Rosie laughed. "You won't be laughing if I catch my death of cold," Gertie told her. "You won't just be playing Cordelia, young lady. You'll be playing Goneril as well!"

Rosie smiled at her. "You'll be all right – it's only water."

Gertie sneezed. "So are you going to wait for me? I'll not stay to watch the show tonight... Once was enough."

Charlie, overhearing her, saved Rosie from replying. "We might go for a walk," he said. "We don't want to get in the way, and there's a boy at the Supper Rooms who hates me."

When they reached the Supper Rooms, Gertie sailed across the road – narrowly avoiding a fast-trotting pony and trap going one way and a brewer's cart the other. Charlie, Rosie and Edie hurried on, hoping that Jago would be too busy to notice them.

When there was no sign, Rosie breathed

a sigh of relief. "Maybe he's not bothered about us anymore."

Edie shook her head. "You ever upset one of them stripy wasps? Stings you over and over to pay you out, and then comes back again for more? That Jago, he's like that. Once he reckons as someone's trod on his toes, he don't stop until he's chopped their feet off."

Charlie looked at her. "Why does he call you names, Edie?"

Edie blushed. "Don't know as I can say."

"I think I can guess," Rosie said. "He asked you out, didn't he, Edie? And you turned him down."

"Didn't want to go walking out with a nasty piece of work like him." Edie stuck her chin in the air. "My gran told me what was right and what was wrong afore I ended up in the workhouse, and I won't never forget what she said. But he ain't worth talking about. And we're here at the Lion ... so what do we do now?"

"We go and sing," Charlie said. "Hey, Edie – can you sing?"

"Croak like a half-baked frog," Edie said cheerfully. "I can whistle a bit, although Cook

said whistling ain't ladylike and didn't let me...
I can take the hat round for you, if you like?"

Charlie pulled off his cap and handed it to
her. "Thank you. Now – let's see what our audience looks like!"

There weren't many customers in the yard
of The Golden Lion. The older men sitting
on the benches, foaming mugs of beer on
the tables in front of them, took no notice as
Charlie and Rosie made their way to the stage;
the young men leaning against the wall were
arguing about politics, and weren't in the least
interested.

It wasn't until Rosie began to sing "Speed
Bonny Boat" that they looked up.

"What's going on?" A tall lad was frowning.
"Caterwauling kids? Put me off my beer, that
will."

His friend elbowed him, grinning. "Jealous,
Doug? Just 'cos you quack like a duck."

"Wanted a bit of peace, that's all," the tall lad
grumbled. "Didn't ask for no concert."

"Nice song, though." His friend was tapping
his foot. "Bit slow, maybe."

As Charlie joined in the chorus, one of the

oldest men began to thump out the beat with his empty mug. Edie grinned at him. "Go for it, Grandpa! That's the way!"

The man grinned back. "Tell 'em to give us something a bit more cheery, love! 'Woodman, Woodman, Spare that Tree'... That's got a bit of body to it, like."

"I know that one," Charlie said. "Come on, Rosie!"

As they swung into the song, accompanied by much banging of tables and a few gruff voices, Sukie came out into the yard to refill the mugs. Unable to resist the catchy tune, she was soon joining in to a roar of approval.

Song after song was sung, and gradually the audience grew bigger. Travellers with bags and cases came in from the station and sat down to listen, and workers from the nearby shops appeared for a rest and a drink. Edie grinned, and began to wander round with Charlie's cap; farthings, half-pennies and pennies were dropped in with a cheery word or smile.

As the evening went on, the crowd began to change: a group of apprentices came in, but instead of joining in they talked loudly amongst themselves. Four or five brewers' lads followed, and when they saw Charlie and Rosie they laughed unpleasantly and shouted out crude suggestions.

Charlie kept singing, but a sudden furious yell brought a shocked silence.

"STOP!" George was scowling heavily. "Sukie! Get back to work right now this minute. And you three: scarper! Nine, I said, and nine I meant. It's no place for you, now – get out of here!"

There was a murmur of disagreement from a few of the men, but most nodded. "Bring the ale out, George. Dry as a desert, we are."

"Aye! Aye! More ale!"

There was more stamping and shouting, but it was fiercer than before and Edie pulled at Rosie's arm. "Best leave now."

Rosie didn't need a second warning; she and Charlie ran after Edie, weaving their way in and out of The Golden Lion's customers. They were almost out of the door when a hand grabbed at Rosie's shoulder, and she squealed.

"No, no, lass ... don't be frightened!" It was the old man who Edie had called 'Grandpa'.

"I've not heard those songs for a long while, and it was grand to hear them again. Here's a six-pence for you – but now be off home. I've got granddaughters your age, and I'd not care to see them out at this time of night."

"Sixpence!" Edie's eyes were very wide as they reached the road. "If I'd knowed you could get sixpence for singing I'd have took lessons!"

Charlie laughed. "Looks like we did well. Let's have a count up..." The cap contained very nearly three shillings, and he beamed at Rosie and Edie. "Pa won't believe it! That has to be enough for posters and flyers, hasn't it?"

"But what about the Hall?" Rosie asked. "Mrs Poskett needs money so she doesn't have to sell it, doesn't she?"

"Sell it?" Edie went white. "But we're taking in lodgers! Them bailiffs – they said we could pay little by little!"

"But it's not up to them anymore... It's that Sleevery man she owes," Charlie told her. "And he wants it now."

Edie clenched her fists. "Well, he ain't going to get it. Not if I has anything to do with it!"

"If we make lots of money we'll share it with

you," Charlie promised, and Rosie took Edie's hand.

"Word of honour," she said. "We'll save the company and the Hall, and then Ma and all the little ones can come and join us ... and we'll all live happily ever after!"

Twenty-one

THE EVENING'S PERFORMANCE AT THE Supper Rooms had been just as much of a triumph as the day before. The applause for Gertie's song had been enthusiastic; Baby, irritated by what he saw as competition, had been spurred into trying even harder, and had dazzled his audience with a cascade of card tricks as well as his usual routine.

Jago, running from kitchen to table with steaming plates of food, had watched eagerly; he could imagine winning impossible amounts of money if he could only learn Baby's ability to slide cards in and out of the pack without being seen. As the evening went on, he grew more and more determined to make Baby his confidant – and should Baby be unwilling ...

well, there were ways to persuade him.

Baby bowed to his audience and retired to Mrs Moore's private parlour. His mother hurried after him, while Mrs Moore remained in the Supper Rooms. A sudden demand for sweet sherry drinks made her realise there was no sugar; calling for Jago, she gave him instructions to run to the corner store to buy a sugarloaf.

"Tell them to put it on the slate," said Mrs Moore. "And you can buy half a pound of butter while you're there."

Jago nodded, nothing loath to leave the hot and steamy supper room, and hurried out. He was just dawdling back from the shop when he saw Edie.

His heart began to flutter wildly in his chest, and he felt breathless. Edie was talking to Charlie and they were looking at each other with what seemed to Jago to be huge admiration. The fluttering in his chest changed to a furious thumping as jealousy and anger misted his sight.

Dumping his purchases on a window ledge, he dashed across the road and fell upon Charlie with flying fists and boots. "Theatre scum!" he yelled. "Workhouse trash!"

Charlie fought back, but Jago had taken him by surprise, and a moment later he was on the ground. Jago stood back to aim a vicious kick at his head, but a whirlwind of black hit him so hard in the stomach that he doubled up, gasping for breath.

Edie rushed him again, this time knocking him over, and he lay beside Charlie moaning and wheezing. She grabbed one of Charlie's arms and Rosie seized the other, and between them they heaved him to his feet.

"Run!" Edie ordered, and run they did. Charlie, his nose bleeding and his left eye gradually closing, was still in a haze, but the girls half-pulled, half-dragged him along until they had gone far enough to be certain they were safe.

As they slowed to a halt, Rosie inspected her brother. "You're a mess, Charlie! Here ... let me clean the blood away."

"OUCH!" Charlie winced, and took the handkerchief for himself. He gave his nose a cursory wipe and looked at Edie. If Jago had been there he would have seen something more than admiration in Charlie's eyes. "Edie ... you floored him! You were amazing!"

Edie blushed. "He weren't fighting fair. Besides, I been wanting to do that awhile now. But he'll cause trouble ... he'll be telling Mrs Moore a tall tale of how it was you as started it." She shook her head. "And she'll believe him. Some folk can't see a liar's a liar, even when they're told that apples is pears and pears is apples."

Charlie grinned and patted his bulging pockets. "Oh well ... who cares about him? We've still got the money."

"Will he try and get you into trouble too, Edie?" Rosie asked anxiously.

"What, and say he was walloped by a girl?" Edie chuckled. "Not likely. It's Charlie he'll be after ... so we'd better watch out. That Jago, he'll be dangerous as a cut-throat razor."

Jago, still unable to stand fully upright, collected the butter and sugar and staggered back to the Supper Rooms. As he went, he was imagining all kinds of revenge – varying from chopping

Charlie's fingers off one by one to boiling him in oil, with many variants in between.

"I'll get him," he promised, "him and all his scummy friends. I'll get them good and proper!"

Mrs Moore was overseeing the end of the meal when Jago reached the kitchen, but to his surprise Baby was standing by the dresser inspecting a bowl of fruit with an air of disapproval.

"Isn't there anything better than this?" he asked Jago. "That old woman said fruit would do me good, but I don't like it. I want ham and eggs. Or roast chicken. Or oysters. Are there any oysters?"

"There's a beef and oyster pie in the larder." This was one of Mrs Moore's specialities, and destined for a meal with friends, but Jago didn't hesitate. "I'll fetch it... But you got to tell me something."

"Pie first." Baby was an able negotiator when it came to his own interests.

Jago nodded and fetched the pie from the top of Mrs Moore's private cupboard.

"Go on then," Baby instructed. "Cut it open. And I want a lot of gravy."

Knife in hand, Jago paused. "How do you do them card tricks?"

Baby hesitated. The intensity of Jago's expression made him uneasy. "I'm not supposed to tell anyone," he said. Then, seeing Jago's face darken, he added, "Magicians aren't allowed to share their tricks except with other magicians, you see. I had to promise. I can't break it. Not even for pie." He gave the pie a last longing look, and began to get up.

"No need to rush off. You don't have to tell me nothing ... I was just asking." Jago sliced the pie in half, and handed Baby a dripping plateful while he considered a different approach. As his companion seized the pie with both hands he asked, as casually as he could, "Know anything about that there theatre lot, do you? At The Golden Lion?"

His mouth too full for speech, Baby shrugged. Several seconds later, and spraying flakes of pastry, he said, "I know mother doesn't like them." He giggled. "She told me someone was sick over their costumes, so they can't work! I think that's funny, don't you?"

Jago was interested. "What kind of costumes?"

Baby waved a sticky hand. "The clothes they dress up in. They have scenery for their plays, as well – that's lots of painted pictures, and props: that's swords and things."

Jago came closer. "So if they ain't got the stuff, they can't work?"

"Of course they can't." Baby was astonished at Jago's ignorance.

This information set Jago thinking. Might it be possible to use Baby to get rid of Charlie? And to do it in some way that would leave the child magician open to a little useful blackmail?

"That singing woman. She's one of them, isn't she?"

"What?" Baby stopped eating to stare at him. "The one who sings about me being magic?" Being entirely self-centred, Baby had never thought to ask where Gertie came from. Now he was interested. She had been applauded, and the only person who deserved applause was Little Baby Bubbles. "Well, I hope she goes back to the Lion and stays there."

"Wouldn't it be better if she went away altogether?" Jago suggested, his weasel eyes even sharper than usual.

Baby considered this idea. "I suppose so."

"As long as she's in Uncaster she'll be warbling away in our supper room." Jago laid his trap. "Mrs Moore, she told me the customers really like her. She says, 'Don't you think she ought to sing more songs, Jago?' That's what she said."

Baby choked on his mouthful. As he coughed and spluttered, Jago went on, "If you ask me, I'd say she'll split the evening soon. Half for her, and half for you..."

This was almost too much; Baby was beginning to shake. Jago, fearing a temper tantrum, hastily added, "But I tells her you're the one they want to see."

Baby, always willing to believe flattery, was soothed. He licked the empty pie plate, and belched loudly. "I've had a very clever idea. I'm going to tell Mrs Moore I'm not going to do another trick until she gets rid of that singing woman."

"I got a better idea." Jago leaned towards Baby. "We get rid of her once and for all. Her and the whole scummy lot – send them scuttling back to where they come from, tails between their legs." Jago paused to check that Baby was listening before he went on, "I'll tell you what – how about me fixing it for you? Then, after they've gone, you can tell her how clever you've been! It'd be a real honour. I mean to say, a nobody like me getting the chance to help a world renowned magician! How lucky is that?"

He gave his companion a sly glance to see if he had gone too far, but Baby was nodding his approval. "That's right," he said. "You're very lucky." Baby blew out his cheeks, glowing with smug self-importance. "After all, you're nothing more than a kitchen boy."

Jago grinned, whilst mentally consigning Baby to a deep dark well. "So that's settled... I'll fix it. But let's keep it as our secret, shall we? Much better that way."

"All right." Baby held out a podgy hand and they shook on the deal. "You fix it – I'm going to go to bed."

Twenty-two

BY THE TIME CHARLIE, EDIE AND ROSIE GOT back to Uncaster Hall, Charlie's eye was purple and completely closed.

Aunt Mags gave a shrill scream when she saw it, and Gertie put her hands over her mouth in horror. "Charlie! What happened?"

Rosie answered for him. "It was that boy from the Supper Rooms. We hadn't done anything – he just rushed at Charlie! He was shouting horrible things – he hit him and he kicked him and knocked him down ... and he'd have kicked him in the head if Edie hadn't punched him!"

"She was a hero," Charlie croaked. "She saved me!"

"T'wasn't nothing to shout about." Edie was

pink with embarrassment. "He got what was coming to him, that's all."

Pa, who was sitting by the stove, turned round to inspect her. "'And though she be but little, she is fierce.' As ever, Shakespeare has a word for the occasion. My dear, how can we thank you?"

"Don't need no thanks," Edie said, and moved a little closer to Rosie. "Friends, they stick up for each other."

Rosie took her hand. "That's right. It is, isn't it, Charlie?"

"Yes." Charlie's nose was throbbing and his eye was sore, but he stood up straight. "One day I'll look after you, Edie."

As Edie blushed an even deeper red, Rosie pulled a handful of coins out of Charlie's pocket and dropped them on the table. "Pa, look what we've got for you!"

Charlie emptied the other pocket. "You can get the flyers printed now."

There was a stunned silence, until Vinnie moved forward to count the money. "Two shillings and eleven pence halfpenny," he announced. "Quite a haul."

"WHAT have you been doing?" Aunt Mags demanded.

Vinnie laughed. "Robbing the Post Office, by the look of it!"

"We didn't!" Rosie was indignant. "We sang songs at The Golden Lion, and Edie took Charlie's cap round."

Pa Pringle leapt to his feet, threw out his arms to embrace this new generous world and hooted with delight. "Music! Sweet music! Did I not tell you music was the key? Mags – dear Mags! Vinnie! Gertie! Our children have shown us the way. The audiences will fall upon us with cries of joy as we reveal the wonders of Shakespeare, accompanied by our merry songs. "

"We could have got more money, but we weren't allowed to stay," Rosie told him. "Everyone started shouting and it got really noisy."

"Could you not sing louder?" Pa asked.

Edie gave him a disapproving glare. "They sang lovely! But a rough old crowd came marching in. Daft lads, they was – lads who only want to hear themselves talking froth and bubble. Wouldn't give a candle for a song, even it were Queen Victoria herself what was singing it."

Aunt Mags was also disapproving. "Fred! Don't be so ungrateful! Look at what they've done for you! And poor Charlie was attacked."

Gertie passed Charlie a damp cloth. "Hold that to your eye," she instructed. "Are you hurt anywhere else?"

Charlie shook his head. "Not really ... only my nose."

Pa pulled his spectacles out of his pocket, and bent down to have a proper look at his son. As he stood up again, his face was very red.

"My poor boy," he said. "The miscreant who did this evil deed must be brought to justice! Tomorrow I shall visit the Supper Rooms, and inform the owner that her servant is a despicable young man—"

"No, Pa." Charlie was shocked by this idea. "You mustn't ... it'll make him worse."

"Edie, my dear! What do you know of this ferocious foe?" Pa asked.

Edie frowned as she thought about Jago. "He's a bad 'un, but that Mrs Moore – she always believes him when he says things ain't his fault. She won't hear a word against him, 'cos he's kind of part of her set-up. She took him in when he was nothing but a babby, and she don't pay him nothing much ... but he gets perks. Won't do any good talking to her."

Pa was not a coward, but he believed in avoiding direct conflict if possible. "Then you must stay away! Charlie, Rosie – do you hear me? And Edie, too. On Saturday we have our first performance, and Cordelia and my fool must be fit and well."

"We'll be fine, Pa." Charlie pointed to the money on the table. "So can we get the flyers and posters printed now?"

"We will order the finest of posters!" Pa beamed. "But as to flyers – behold!" And he pointed to a pile of handwritten papers on the chair beside him.

Rosie picked one up. "'Come and be thrilled, fascinated and delighted by the Steam Whistle Theatre Company, straight from the heart of London. A king in torment, a daughter lost ... the tale will be told at The Golden Lion on Saturday, and every night thereafter at the hour of nine-thirty.' Pa ... couldn't we begin a bit earlier?"

"Earlier? No, no, my darling. There may well be those who wish to indulge in both varieties of magic in just one evening, you see. I have consulted with Gertie, and she assures me that the child magician has escaped his chains by nine – so I confidently expect an enormous crowd to come hurrying hotfoot to the Lion for a second helping of entertainment."

"And I can go on singing," Gertie put in. "A shilling a week is a shilling a week. Always comes in handy!"

"Oh..." Rosie looked at Charlie, then at Edie.

She was going to protest further, but Aunt Mags held up her hand. "Bed! Charlie, you look dreadful, and Rosie, you've got big black circles under your eyes. And Edie, forgive me dear – but you should be in bed too!"

At the other end of the high street, Mrs Moore was deep in thought. Bookings for the next few days were excellent, and her new iron safe was already pleasantly full.

Nevertheless she was not happy; she was beginning to have doubts about a number of things, and one of them was Jago. She was, in her own cold way, fond of him, but she had had to defend him more and more over the past few months. It hardly seemed logical that the fights, missing items and complaints of damaged property were always someone else's fault.

And then there was Baby. Her private parlour was no longer hers; he spent all day there, eating and sleeping. Occasionally he practised his card tricks, or spun coins in and out of glass bottles, but mostly he was grunting in her very own armchair. As for his mother ... Mrs Moore shuddered. She knew, beyond the shadow of a doubt, that Mrs Snicket was an accomplished thief, and if the Supper Rooms got a bad reputation she would be ruined.

"I'll give him one more week," she decided. "And maybe I'll ask that Gracegirdle woman if she'd care to sing a couple more songs tonight. If she goes down well I might ask her to take over after he's gone – she got a good round of applause yesterday, and after all, music's what we're best known for."

And with this thought, Mrs Moore lit her candle and retired to bed.

Twenty-three

EDIE WAS UP EARLY THE FOLLOWING morning; Arabella's letter was on the hall table, ready to take to the post, and she picked it up. *I'll save my lady a walk*, she told herself – and ran out into the sunshine.

Mr Tramways had just opened up, but even so Edie wasn't his first customer; Olio Sleevery was leaning on the counter, sorting through a bundle of papers. He sneered when he saw Edie and turned his back on her.

"Got a letter to post, Mr T," Edie said. "Letter from Mrs Poskett."

Olio Sleevery did not turn round, but he paused in his sorting.

"Pop it on the counter," Mr Tramways told her. "Man'll be here to collect any minute now."

As Edie thanked him and skipped out into the sunshine again, Olio Sleevery gave the letter a sly glance. Seeing the name his gaze sharpened, and with a swift movement of his hand knocked it to the floor.

"How careless of me," he said, and as he picked it up he deftly exchanged it for one of his own. Putting Arabella's letter in his pocket, he finished his business and left the Post Office with no word of thanks. Mr Tramways snorted his disapproval, then scooped up the letters and put them in the collection bag.

Once outside, Olio Sleevery scanned Arabella's impassioned plea to her sister-in-law and whistled through his teeth. "So! Thinks she'll go begging, does she? 'If not for me, dear Jocasta, then for the children...' Ha!" He crumpled up the letter and tossed it away. "No help now, Mrs Arabella Poskett. Not a single penny. I've a buyer waiting who'll pay me nine hundred pounds for your home ... and I'll not lose that chance!"

He began to walk away, but stopped as a thought came to him. What if someone else saw the advertisement for a large house in

Uncaster? Swinging on his heel, he strode back to the Post Office.

"I'll take the rest of those." He picked up the remaining copies of *The Free Press*.

Mr Tramways bristled. "You will not! That's a paper for anyone who wants one."

"And I'm wanting them." Olio scowled and marched out, and there was nothing the old man could do to stop him.

Rosie, Gertie and the bruised and battered Charlie were already in the kitchen when Aunt Mags came marching in, Edie in her wake. When she announced the morning's menu, only Rosie looked cheerful.

"Bread and water?" she said. "We can pretend we're prisoners!"

Arabella, coming through the door, heard her. "Prisoners? Oh no, Rosie dear! Is staying here as bad as that?"

Rosie looked embarrassed. "It was Aunt Mags saying about the bread and water," she said. "We love it here. Truly! Don't we, Charlie?"

Charlie nodded. "Best lodgings we've ever

had," he said. "Hope we can stay here a good long time."

Arabella suppressed a sigh and Edie gave her an anxious glance. Charlie, unnoticing, went on: "Rosie's never had a little theatre to sleep in before!"

Seeing Arabella's puzzled expression, Rosie explained, "He means our curtained bed."

"Oh!" Arabella's face cleared. "The four-poster! There's an even bigger one in the blue bedroom, but we don't use it because the curtains rotted away." She sat down and took a letter from her pocket.

As she began to read, Pa came puffing through the door. "Good morning, my dear companions! And what a busy day it will be. Rosie, Charlie and Edie too, if her duties will allow – you will spend the day handing out our most wonderfully handwritten flyers."

He bowed to Arabella, but she was frowning over her correspondence and didn't notice.

"I will take it upon myself to find a printer, and once we have posters – paid for by the talented younger members of our little company, and I include you in my description, dear Edie – we will paste them here, there, and everywhere." He stopped, and gave the younger members a considering look. "And as for tonight ... perhaps more singing, my darlings? Followed, of course, by a loud and clear announcement that this coming Saturday, finally and at last, the Steam Whistle Theatre Company will be presenting that much anticipated and longed for production ... *The Death of King Lear*!"

He stood back waiting for enthusiastic agreement, but Aunt Mags merely nodded. "So we have a couple of days to get ready?"

Pa beamed at her. "Correct, dear Mags."

Before Aunt Mags could answer, Arabella gave a sharp exclamation. Everyone at the table turned to look at her, and she flushed. "I'm so sorry, that was unpardonably rude ... but Aunt Jocasta is unbearable! She says she only now understands the depths to which the Poskett family has sunk – oh, whatever have my darlings been telling her?" She flung the letter down on the table, and wiped her eyes. "I did so hope they might be missing their mother, just a little..."

"I'm sure they are – in their own way." Aunt Mags tried to be comforting.

"Absence will surely make the hearts grow fonder," Pa declared. "Dear lady, you have been kindness itself to us poor strolling players. Without your hospitality we would have been lost: quite lost."

Once again Edie glanced at Arabella, but nothing was said and Pa settled down to his dry bread with every indication of satisfaction.

The day went on: Edie decided she would stay at home to help with the household duties, and to keep an eye on Arabella, although she did not say as much; Charlie and Rosie went out with their bundle of flyers with Vinnie to help them.

Meeting Pa later, they were delighted to be able to tell him that every flyer had found a home. Pa, after congratulating them, had good news of his own – he had found a small printing works that was happy to do a rush job, and posters would be ready that afternoon.

He walked back to the Hall with his children, expounding the glories of Theatre and Music as they went. Even the discovery of a number of screwed-up flyers lying in the road did not depress him.

"They'll have taken note of the time and place," he said. "Have faith, my children! Talent will out!"

Rosie, walking silently at his side, was not so sure. She had been secretly pleased when George called time at The Golden Lion the night before; the latecomers had scared her. How would they feel when their drinking was interrupted by a play? Or would they take no notice, and behave as if King Lear and his daughters weren't there? If they were a failure, what would happen then?

Rosie's stomach tied itself into knots as she wondered. No money would mean they were stuck in Uncaster, and the thought of not seeing Ma made the knots tighten painfully.

"Pa," she said, "what if we can't go home? Will Ma ever be able to come here?"

Pa, interrupted in the middle of a monologue about Hamlet, looked at her in surprise. "Don't you go worrying, Rosie pet. We're at the very beginning of our adventure! And we'll be sending for Ma in no time at all."

"But what if they don't like us?" Rosie insisted. "What if nobody wants to see *King Lear*, and we don't make any money?"

"Not want to see *Lear*?" In Pa's view, this was an impossibility. "My love – what are you saying? Of course there'll be money! And soon we'll be one big happy family again."

Choosing his words carefully, Charlie asked, "Pa ... what would happen if we weren't able to stay at Uncaster Hall?"

"Ods bodkins!" Pa threw up his hands. "Whence has happiness fled? Where is hope? Where is positivity?" He seized Rosie and Charlie in a bearlike embrace, and danced them along the road until they were laughing. "Trust me, my darlings! All will be well!"

As he let them go, Charlie put his arm round Rosie's shoulders. "We're singing tonight, re-member ... and that'll be another three shillings. Three more tomorrow, as well. There's money coming in already, Rosie. Pa's right: it'll be fine."

But, when the evening came, it wasn't at all fine. When Charlie, Rosie and Edie arrived at The Golden Lion, Sukie met them with a grave face.

"Not tonight, ducks," she said. "We had com-plaints, see ... and George, he thinks he lost sales. The old boys liked it, though, so you could come back tomorrow for half an hour or so in the afternoon. George wouldn't say no to that."

"Couldn't we just have ten minutes?" Charlie begged – but Sukie was adamant.

As the three children walked away, the mournful sound of a train whistle echoed in the evening air; there was the distant *chuff-chuff-chuff* as the last train of the day set off back to London.

"It's all going wrong." Rosie was near to tears. "We'll never be able to go home."

Charlie was frowning. "It's not fair. She told us we could sing and we really need the money. I'm beginning to wonder why we ever came here."

Rosie gave herself a mental shake. "At least we've made a friend. We'll always be friends, won't we, Edie?"

"Yes." Edie agreed with an emphatic nod. She pointed to the bright new poster on the wall at the end of the street. "*Ooooh!* Looks wonderful, don't it?"

The poster did look appealing, and Charlie cheered up a little. "Maybe Pa's right and we'll get an audience."

"Just as long as they aren't like those apprentices, last night." Rosie shuddered. "Did you hear what they were shouting?"

"I tried not to," Charlie said – and then, "Look! There's another poster! Pa was really busy this afternoon, wasn't he? Maybe it'll be all right without our extra money after all."

"Will we come back tomorrow?" Edie asked.

Charlie was doubtful. "I think Pa wants an all-day rehearsal... Hey! You'll be able to watch, Edie!"

"I never did see a play before!" Edie was thrilled, and as she and Charlie turned the corner into the high street she took his arm and began asking him what he would be doing, and what everyone else did to make the play work.

Rosie, keeping an anxious eye out for Jago, walked behind them. There was a lump in her throat, and a hollow feeling in her stomach. *It's all horrible*, she told herself. *Edie's the only nice thing here.* She sniffed, and rubbed her eyes. *I do so wish we could go home to Ma, or that Ma could come here. I do miss her so...*

Twenty-five

THE MAGICIAN AT THE SUPPER ROOMS WAS also unhappy, but for very different reasons. Eating a whole beef and oyster pie had resulted in serious indigestion and at 3 a.m. he had been certain that he was dying – Mrs Snicket had insisted on sending for the doctor, and a sleepy Jago was forced to struggle out to knock on Doctor Harris's door. Doctor Harris had been far too dismissive of Baby's condition for Mrs Snicket's liking; he had taken one look, prescribed Cockle's Antibilious Pills and stomped away muttering about wasted time.

Baby went on wailing until the morning, when at last he fell into an exhausted sleep. Mrs Snicket also slept; Mrs Moore, suffering from a splitting headache and an exceptionally bad temper, got up and went down to the kitchen, slamming doors as she went. When Mrs Snicket appeared later in the morning to request a hot tisane for darling Baby she was told, in no uncertain terms, to make it herself.

Baby himself appeared well after midday. He flung himself into Mrs Moore's chair and put his feet on her spotless, linen-covered table, knocking a small china jug into the grate where it shattered into a thousand pieces. Mrs Moore gave a sharp exclamation of annoyance, which Baby ignored.

"I can't perform tonight," he announced. "I'm too tired. You'll have to cancel my show."

"I'll do no such thing!" The pain in Mrs Moore's head was excruciating and it was all she could do not to slap Baby. "We're sold out, and I'm not in the habit of letting my customers down."

Unused to such treatment, Baby turned purple. "You can't make me! I won't!"

Mrs Moore was about to snap back at him when Mrs Snicket came hurrying in, alarmed by the sound of raised voices but smiling her merriest smile. "Birds living together in one little nest ought always to agree! Now ... do tell. What's the problem?"

"She won't listen." Baby pointed at Mrs Moore. "She says I've got to do the show, and I *won't*. I'm too tired."

His mother was all too used to Baby's tantrums. "Of course you're tired, my dearest darling. Such a poorly thing – I shouldn't think you had a wink of sleep last night!" She put an arm round his shoulder and, making sure he couldn't see or hear her, she mouthed at Mrs Moore, *Leave him to me!*

Mrs Moore snorted her disapproval and stamped out of the parlour. Baby's mother sat down and pulled her enormous child onto her knee, murmuring soothing noises as she did so. She could hardly breathe, but the discomfort would be worth it if she could persuade him to perform.

Baby initially resisted, but gradually he relaxed and, after much stroking and petting and flattery, muttered that he might manage half an hour. Mrs Snicket, who had lost all feeling in her legs, gave him a loving kiss.

"Let's go and have a little look at your box

of tricks," she suggested, "and you can choose what you would like to do."

To this Baby agreed, and the two of them got to their feet – Mrs Snicket with some difficulty.

Baby looked at her in disgust. "You're getting old," he said. "I need a new assistant. Someone young, not an old woman like you."

His mother gave a tinkling laugh, whilst surreptitiously rubbing her knees. "I expect you're right, precious one. We'll have to see what we can do, won't we?"

Baby grunted. The adventures of the night before had left him with a curious mixture of suspicion and admiration for the kitchen boy. "I want Jago to help me tonight."

"I'm not sure Mrs Moore will be able to spare him..." Mrs Snicket began, then swiftly changed direction as Baby's brow darkened. "But of course I'll see what I can arrange!"

They found Mrs Moore in the Supper Rooms, supervising the cleaning of the tables. All three kitchen boys were there, and to Mrs Snicket's surprise Jago's employer raised no objections when it was suggested he might like to assist Baby. Mrs Moore was, in fact, hugely relieved; she had been worrying about the evening as a cancellation would not only mean returning money, but also lead to a good deal of ill feeling.

"I presume that means you'll be performing after all," she said. "You can cut five minutes off your show if you're feeling poorly; I'm going to ask Miss Gracegirdle to sing three songs this evening. The customers like her."

This comment made Baby blink. Should he throw another tantrum? While he was trying to decide, Jago saw an opportunity and came sidling up to whisper in his ear.

"What did I tell you! Don't say nothing. I'll sort it!"

Mrs Snicket was unable to hear what Jago had said, but she saw Baby nod. Grateful that he wasn't making a fuss, she turned to Mrs Moore with her most gracious smile. "Three songs? How thoughtful of you. Just for tonight, of course – and I'm assuming there'll be no alteration in our financial agreement?"

"We'll see." Mrs Moore did not return her smile. Instead, she swept away to rearrange a line of benches.

Deciding she had won, Mrs Snicket tried to take Baby's arm but he shook her off.

"I'm going to show Jago what to do," he said. "You can go away."

Jago gave her a sly wink. "It's all right, Missus."

"Goodness me! How fast my Baby is growing up! But boys will always be boys," Mrs Snicket trilled – but as she was unable to think of any excuse to stay, she did as she was told and left.

Baby, with an efficiency that Jago hadn't expected, began to demonstrate how to keep the tricks in order, and how it was important that the chains were wrapped round his chest as he was breathing in.

Jago listened carefully and Baby gave him a patronising pat on the back. "Good. I asked for you, you know ... so you'd better do as I say."

"It'll be my pleasure," Jago lied.

The evening began well. Gertie was startled to be told she was to sing three songs, but pleased. She began with "The Boy I Love is Up in the Balcony", and was greeted with shouts of approval and much banging of forks on tables.

Baby, behind the curtains, began to scowl. When her next song met with an equally enthusiastic response, he decided to take matters into his own hands. Ignoring Mrs Moore's warning glare he burst through the curtains, pushed Gertie off the stage, and swept off his silver top hat.

As the flowers sprang up he waited for the usual applause – but there was only a faint murmur, swiftly followed by laughter. Gertie was pirouetting her way in between the tables, smiling and waving as she made her way out of the room.

"That's ever such a lovely lady," said an admiring voice, and Baby's scowl deepened. As Jago joined him on stage, he snatched up a pack of cards and began to shuffle them angrily. The diners, now attacking their fish, watched with interest.

If they were hoping to see the child magician lose his temper on stage, however, they were disappointed. The next few tricks went smoothly, and the response began to warm; by the time the entrée was being served even Baby had begun to relax.

In all his fifteen years Jago had never been applauded by anyone, let alone an audience, and it went straight to his head. Glowing with pride after the show, he slapped Baby on the back as they walked down the corridor that led to Mrs Moore's kitchen.

"I did well, didn't I?" he boasted. "Did you see them clapping me when I did those chains? They clapped really loud!"

Baby had indeed noticed the extra applause, and had not been impressed. Jago had been playing to the audience: he had pretended to puff and pant as he pulled the chains tight, and this had gone down much too well in Baby's opinion. The role of an assistant was to assist, and under no circumstances upstage the star. Had Jago been suitably grateful and humble he might have been forgiven ... but arrogance was not to be borne.

"You were hopeless," he said crossly, "and I don't want you tomorrow. I should have known a stupid kitchen boy wasn't going to be any good. And I don't want anything to do with your silly ideas, either – I'm too famous."

For a moment, Jago was speechless. Then his

heart began to thunder so hard he could feel it pounding against the walls of his chest. He slid away without a word.

Baby shrugged and headed for Mrs Moore's parlour, where he flung himself into his favourite chair. His mother flew to his side and soon he was attacking a plate piled high with thick slices of beef, ham and chicken.

In the kitchen, Jago was pacing up and down, muttering and swearing. The other kitchen boys gave him a wide berth; when he grabbed his coat and slammed out into the street no one dared to make any comment.

Once outside he set off at a run for The Golden Lion, where apprentice lads greeted him – as did a small group furtively conversing in a corner, hats pulled low over their eyes.

One sidled up to Jago. "Got anything for us? Bit of beef? One of them pies?"

"Not tonight," Jago told him, and he slithered in between the tables until he reached the stage. Five cheery farmers were sitting there with their mugs of beer bellowing at each other in voices used to wide open spaces. They took no notice of Jago as he circled round, inspecting the Steam Whistle Theatre Company's performance area.

The shed interested him. Peering through a crack in the door, he could see two large wicker hampers emblazoned with the company's name. He was annoyed to find them protected by a heavy padlock; after a moment's thought, he slipped behind the shed to see if there was another way inside. A loose board was promising: a quick heave and a tug, and it came away. A wriggle, a squirm, and Jago was in ...

... and his pent up anger with both Baby and Charlie *exploded* as he ripped and tore at the contents of the baskets. Painted backdrops were unrolled and stamped on, swords snapped in two, shields and helmets dented, ghostly papier maché heads trashed and trails of artificial flowers pulled apart: nothing was left untouched.

Then, finding a bucket of old whitewash on a shelf, he went to work with an enthusiasm that would have astonished Mrs Moore.

By the time he had damaged, destroyed or demolished every single item, Jago's anger had died down to a slow simmer; he looked round at the wreckage with intense satisfaction before squeezing back out.

Choosing a moment when the farmers were loudly discussing the relative virtues of Swaledale as against Wensleydale sheep, he walked casually past and into the heart of the shouting, arguing, beer-swilling crowd.

Twenty-six

FRIDAY DAWNED, BRIGHT AND SUNNY; THE hens had laid and breakfast was a jolly affair. There was even butter to go with the bread – Aunt Mags had been out the day before, and set up an arrangement with the local grocer.

The curtains were pronounced dry and so were the company's costumes: the only casualty was the dress Rosie wore as Cordelia. Hearing it had shrunk beyond recognition, Arabella offered to take her up to the attic. "You should see what's up there," she said. "Dresses belonging to Henry's mother, grandmother and even his great-grandmother! They never threw anything away."

"Quite right," Aunt Mags said approvingly.

Rosie followed Arabella up the flights of

stairs, and Edie came too for company. Rows of dresses were hung on dusty wooden racks, and there were more folded into large leather trunks or heaped on the floor under thick cotton dust-sheets. Rosie hadn't been looking for long when she gave an excited squeak, and pounced on an old fashioned blue dress. "Can I wear this?"

"Blue's your colour, dear." Arabella surveyed the collection. "I don't remember there being quite so many. It seems such a shame that they're not being used."

Edie was tenderly smoothing the skirt of a red velvet gown lying crumpled on the floor. "These must be worth a fortune, Ma'am. What about giving them to Miss Twillfit? She's always making new dresses from old ones. She'd pay you for them, too."

Arabella gave a little gasp. "Edie! Would she really? Will you ask her?"

"I'll go today, Ma'am," Edie promised, then hesitated. "What time is you doing the play, Rosie? I really, REALLY wants to see that."

"About two o'clock, I think," Rosie said. "Pa and Aunt Mags are taking the curtains to The Golden Lion this morning, and they'll bring

241

back a few props we need for a full dress rehearsal in the drawing room ... if that's all right with you, Mrs Poskett."

Arabella nodded. "Of course, dear." She bent down and picked up the gown Edie had been admiring. "Edie, when you go to see Miss Twillfit take this with you. I'll give you a note explaining you have my permission, and suggesting perhaps she should come here to have a look for herself."

In the drawing room, Vinnie, Charlie and Gertie were moving chairs into rows, as if they were expecting an audience. "It gives us the right atmosphere," Rosie told Edie. "Lots of people stand to watch, but it's nice if there's chairs as well."

Edie nodded, her face serious. "Can I sit on a seat?"

"You can sit in the front row." Charlie grinned at her. "Did you know I play the fool? I keep the king company when he gets thrown out of his palace."

"What do the others do?" Edie wanted to know.

"Pa is Lear, of course, and Rosie's Cordelia. Gertie is Goneril, Aunt Mags is Regan and Vinnie is lots of different dukes ... mostly Gloucester." Charlie clutched his head and gave a realistic groan. "He has his eyes put out in the play, so he's blind."

Edie's eyes widened. "That's not nice. I don't have to watch them doing it, do I?"

Charlie laughed. "Not in Pa's version."

"I'll sit next to you when they don't need me to play the piano," Arabella said, "and we can be scared together."

This pleased Edie, and she rewarded Arabella with one of her beaming smiles.

An hour later Edie was walking towards Miss Twillfit's little shop with the red velvet dress in a bundle under her arm. She waved to Mr Tramways, who was standing outside his Post Office smoking his pipe in the sunshine, and gave a little skip of happiness as she thought how her life had changed. The Honourable Henry had done at least one good thing in his life, she decided; he had rescued her from the harshest of lives as a kitchen skivvy.

"I got friends, I got friends!" she sang, and she skipped again.

Miss Twillfit, at first decidedly chilly, became a different person after reading Arabella's note. She read it twice, then took the dress and laid it out on her counter.

"Beautiful," she sighed. "Absolutely beautiful. And there are more like this?"

Edie nodded. "Loads, miss. And all kinds of colours! Some are all lacy, and some are velvety with lots of bows, and some have got little tiny beads sewn all over them."

"I will visit very soon," Miss Twillfit declared, her cheeks pink with excitement. "Thank you, Edie!" She pulled out a drawer and chose four scarlet ribbons. "Here ... a present for you. It's not every day I have such wonderful news!"

"Thank you, miss! Thank you very, very much!" Edie was breathless. "But is it all right if I gives two to my friend Rosie?"

"They're yours to do with as you wish," Miss Twillfit said.

Edie, in a state of ecstasy, left the shop with a cheerful wave. Seeing Pa and Aunt Mags approaching she ran towards them ... and stopped.

Shortly before his unfortunate demise, the Honourable Henry had invited a friend to visit him by air balloon. Edie had been enthralled by the arrival of the huge red and yellow globe; she had never seen anything quite as magnificently buoyant since, until she met Pa. But now he was like the balloon after the gas had escaped, leaving a sagging empty bag.

"What is it? What's happened?" Edie chose to ask Aunt Mags, who was scarlet with rage – but still fiercely upright.

"Trashed," Aunt Mags said tersely. "Everything's gone. All our props, the scenery, the screens … everything. Someone got into the shed and destroyed every single thing in there."

There was nothing Edie could say – she walked beside Aunt Mags silently, down the high street and in through the gates of Uncaster Hall.

Through the front door, down the hallway and into the drawing room they went, where Rosie, wearing the blue dress from the attic, spun round and round in front of them.

"Look, Pa! Look—" she saw their faces, and froze. "Pa! What is it?" And then, thinking of the worst possible thing that could ever happen, she asked in a trembling voice, "Has something happened to Ma?"

This terrible thought brought Pa back into the real world with a jolt. He managed a half-smile, and patted Rosie's arm. "No, pet. Ma's fine."

It was Aunt Mags who told the assembled company about the destruction of all their theatrical possessions. "Everything's covered in whitewash, too," she said. "It was as if someone hated us so much they couldn't make it bad enough by smashing and trashing everything – they had to pour paint on it as well."

Arabella gave a gasp of horror. "But that's a terrible thing to do!"

"George said someone must have climbed over the wall after everyone had gone home last night. He said nobody could have done it while the Lion was open ... they'd have been seen or heard." Aunt Mags sighed wearily as she sat down. "And he said we were nothing but trouble, and we weren't welcome. So we haven't got a venue any more, even if we could replace what we've lost."

Charlie, who had been silently taking in the horror of the situation, came forward. "So what do we do now?"

"We'll have to go home," Rosie said, but Pa shook his head.

"No money for tickets, pet. We're sunk." He looked at Arabella, his large round face white and strained. "I'm so sorry, Ma'am. We won't be able to pay you. We'll move out at the end of the week."

Rosie stared at him. "But where will we go if we can't go home? Pa?"

"Hush, pet," Pa said, and he put his arm round her.

"Couldn't we stay here?" Rosie was trembling as she turned to Arabella. "Just for a little while?"

Arabella had tears in her eyes. "I'm so sorry. Unless Aunt Jocasta helps us – and I'm afraid I don't think it's very likely – Uncaster Hall won't be mine much longer. But while it is, of course you are all most welcome to remain."

There was a lengthy silence, before Vinnie said, "Sounds as if we've all been rowing in leaking boats ... and now we're sinking." He gave a mirthless laugh. "Watch out for sharks. They'll be swirling round any minute now, you mark my words."

"Be quiet, Vinnie!" Gertie was shocked. She pulled a shilling out of her pocket and handed it to Pa. "Here's what that old skinflint at the Supper Rooms gave me. It's not much, I know – but it's better than nothing."

Pa took a deep breath. "Thank you, Gertie." He breathed again, and a little colour came back to his face. "You remind me that we are a group with talent, with skills, with flair. We may yet be able to survive this tragedy—"

"It's no good, Fred." Vinnie was hunched over, the picture of defeated misery. "We're done for."

"NO!" Edie stamped her foot; her eyes were sparking. "You ain't done for 'til you're dead! That's what my gran told me – and my gran, she was ALWAYS right!" She pointed to the chairs, and the empty space that was the stage area. "Why can't you do the play here? It's all got ready!"

Vinnie sighed. "It's not that easy, Edie. We need to get a paying audience, you see—"

"I knows that!" Edie stamped her foot again. "I ain't silly! But you can get one if you try! Them posters – change them! March up and down the street! And that Jago, he didn't get your costumes, did he? They was here ... so wear them! Uncaster folk, they've been dying to see what's what in this place for years and years, nosy blighters that they are. They'll come. Stake my life, they will!"

"And so they will!" Pa roared. He was visibly swelling back to his normal circumference, and his eyes were shining like stars. "We are saved ... saved by the wisdom of our precious Edie—"

"Just a minute, Fred." Aunt Mags was on her feet. She was smiling, but cautiously. "Isn't there something you and Edie are forgetting? This is Uncaster Hall and it belongs to Mrs Poskett. We can't just take over."

"But you can!" Arabella clasped Aunt Mags' hands. "I beg of you, please do!" A shadow crossed her face. "It may only be for a few days – Mr Sleevery is pressing me for my decision – but it would give me such pleasure if I could help you."

"Then we are agreed." Pa swept her a low bow. "And we will forever remain in your debt, dear lady."

Aunt Mags nodded. "Fred's spoken for us all. Thank you."

Vinnie was stroking his chin: always a sign he was thinking. "Gertie ... when you're at the Supper Rooms tonight, you must tell everyone there's a performance here tomorrow. If Mrs Moore doesn't like it, it won't matter. We won't be around to bother her much longer."

Gertie chuckled. "That'll upset the child magician no end!" She glanced at Charlie. "Forgot to tell you ... Jago was helping him last night, instead of his mother. That should stop him from hanging around in the street."

Charlie laughed. "I'll be all right as long as I've got Edie to protect me." He turned to grin at Edie, only to find she wasn't there. By the time he reached the front door to look for her, Edie was out of sight, running up the high street as fast as she could go.

Twenty-seven

ELIZA SNICKET WAS HAVING A LEISURELY morning. Baby was still asleep and rather than descend to order her luncheon, she decided to take the opportunity of a quiet moment to count the contents of her purse and the metal box under her bed.

As Baby had not required her services on stage the evening before, she had taken the opportunity to join the audience. A prosperous looking gentleman had caught her eye; entranced by the magic, he had hardly noticed when Mrs Snicket sat down next to him. It had almost been too easy to remove his snakeskin wallet and silver watch. For her own amusement, she had returned the empty wallet.

Now she added the contents to her previous takings, and gave a contented sigh. They could certainly move to York ... but when? She gazed out of the window as her thoughts floated idly amongst various pleasant possibilities.

A neat little trap pulled by two glossy ponies went past at a smart trot, and she wondered if it might be possible to acquire a carriage of her own. Smiling, she imagined acknowledging admiring glances as she was driven round the cobbled streets. A large man was crossing the road towards the Supper Rooms, and she practised a gracious wave.

He looked up – and Mrs Snicket dropped to her hands and knees as she recognized her prey from the night before. Had he seen her? She thought not. Was he looking for her?

Her thoughts whirling like confetti in the wind, Eliza Snicket pulled her suitcase out, pushed it away again ... then pulled it back. What should she do? If he was coming to accuse her, he must even now be on the point of knocking. She tiptoed to her door and listened.

There was no sound of a knock, no sound of voices. She crept back to the window ... and heaved a sigh of relief: the man was walking past.

Kicking the case, she scolded herself for being so quick to lose her nerve. "It was just a coincidence. That's all it was! But Uncaster's a small place, a very small place. It's time Baby and I moved on. Mrs Moore will be disappointed, of course, but it would be wise. We can afford it and that's a blessing."

In the parlour below, Mrs Moore was also making decisions. "How much longer should I let that dreadful woman stay? The boy may be good at magic, but he's a spoilt fool." The now familiar conflict between greed and sense gripped her. "Shall I tell them to go right now? Or give them one more night? And maybe Saturday? Saturday's always very popular and we've sold a lot of tickets ... and then I could ask Miss Gracegirdle if she'd like a formal engagement."

Greed won out and Mrs Moore determined she would speak to Eliza Snicket to inform her that Baby's last performance would take place on Saturday. She sat down and, deciding a glass of wine would be appropriate, rang her bell for Jago.

He appeared almost at once, looking unusually pleased with himself. "Got a bit of news, Miss," he said. "That Steam Whistle lot – they'll be off back to London soon. The Lion's chucked them out ... damaged the shed, they did, and threw paint around as well."

Expecting his news to be greeted with pleasure, Jago was disconcerted to see Mrs Moore frown. "What do you mean? They haven't put on a single performance yet."

Jago sniggered. "And they never will. Got none of the stuff they need: it all got trashed."

Mrs Moore stared at him. "Trashed? Are you saying they destroyed their own property?"

A sudden realisation that he might be on shaky ground made Jago swerve. "I didn't say that, Miss! I'm just saying what I heard!"

Before Mrs Moore could make any further enquiries, Eliza Snicket appeared, exuding warmth and friendliness. "Dearest Mrs Moore! And the handsome Jago! How are you both this fine morning?"

Hoping for a more enthusiastic response,

Jago repeated his news about the Steam Whistle Theatre Company – only to be rebuffed a second time as Mrs Snicket gave a little scream, and threw up her hands. "Such a dreadful thing!"

Baffled, Jago looked from one woman to the other. "Ain't you glad?"

"Oh, Jago! My darling Baby never needs to worry about competition!" Mrs Snicket gave Jago a warning wink. "And I have some sad, sad news. Baby and I won't be able to stay much longer ... he's so in demand! My dear Mrs Moore, I hope you can find it in your heart to forgive us – but we must leave you on Sunday."

Despite this fitting with her plans, Mrs Moore was irritated that it was Mrs Snicket who had initiated the break. "I'm not at all sure that's convenient," she said coldly. "I shall lose a great deal of goodwill as tickets have already been sold for next week."

Eliza Snicket wavered: was she being unnecessarily anxious?

But Mrs Moore continued, "Of course, you must do as seems best to you. I don't wish to stand in your way. I shall ask Miss Gracegirdle to take Baby's place." She tossed her head. "She seems to suit my customers very well."

Jago, whose plans for forcing Baby to give up his secrets were falling apart before his eyes, gulped. "But she won't be here! Like I said, Miss! They'll be off, soon as winking!"

Mrs Moore gave the kitchen boy a glacial stare. "If I offer Miss Gracegirdle a position, she will have no reason to leave. And I can't see why it's of any interest to you, Jago."

This was pouring salt in the wound: not only was Baby going, but the theatre company might stay. Before Jago could raise any further objections, there was a loud knocking and Mrs Snicket jumped.

"A visitor, dear Mrs Moore! Not for me, I'm certain. I shall leave you in peace." And she scurried away until she was out of sight. Hiding behind a convenient cupboard, she waited to see who was at the door.

"See who that is, Jago," Mrs Moore ordered. Jago did as he was told – and found Edie, eyes blazing, fists clenched, and trembling with rage.

"It was you!" she shouted and she stamped her foot. "It was you as did it, Jago Wilson! It ain't no use saying as you didn't—"

Jago shut the door and leant against it as Edie pounded wildly on the knocker, still shouting, "It was you! It was you!"

Inside, Mrs Moore came hurrying to see what the noise was – and Jago slid the bolt to keep the door shut. Edie's attack had shaken him and he was finding it hard to retain his air of innocence.

"She's mad, Miss. Raving. Someone should lock her up!"

It was all too easy to hear Edie's accusations, and Mrs Moore raised her eyebrows. "What is it that you're supposed to have done, Jago? Who IS that girl?"

Jago shrugged. "Workhouse scum." A sly thought came to him. "She wants to be my girl – but I don't want nothing to do with dirt like that. Makes her madder 'n' a raging bull."

"She seems to have stopped now." Mrs Moore was right. Silence had fallen; Jago peered through the letterbox.

"She's talking to a man," he reported. "Saw him here last night. And the policeman's there, too."

Behind the cupboard, Mrs Snicket went very pale.

"If that girl comes shrieking here again I'm reporting her," Mrs Moore said sharply. "Now, get back to the kitchen. And if I find you've been causing trouble there'll be extremely serious consequences. Do you understand me?"

However much he tried, Jago had never been able to overcome a childhood fear of Mrs Moore. He nodded and disappeared, and Mrs Moore went to find her own glass of wine.

Outside, Constable Grimshaw was frowning. "I could arrest you for breach of the peace, young lady. Hollering and hooting outside a respectable establishment!"

"Respectable, constable?" The large man beside him sounded tetchy. "I had my pocket picked here last night and this young lady quite evidently has a serious complaint. Did they steal from you too, girl?"

"Me?" Edie shook her head. "It's that rat of a boy what's ruined everything! EVERYTHING!" She shook her fist at the Supper Rooms. "I hates him!"

"Now, now, Miss." Constable Grimshaw put a heavy hand on Edie's shoulder. "You run away home. Live in the tenements, do you?"

"I lives in Uncaster Hall," Edie said proudly. "I works for Mrs Poskett."

The large man raised his eyebrows. "Really? I understood Uncaster Hall was uninhabited?" He drew a letter from inside his waistcoat. "Yes. As I thought. Uncaster Hall, currently unoccupied, for sale at reasonable terms. Property of Mr O. Sleevery. You're telling fibs, girl."

"No I ain't!" Edie's eyes flashed. "I never tells lies!"

Constable Grimshaw coughed. *Ahem.* The girl's right, Sir. Been in the Poskett family for years."

The large man looked again at his letter. "Been in the family for years, you say? I find that information interesting. I'm here as an agent for the North Western Railway Company, and it seems we have been misinformed. I apologise, young lady—"

But Edie had wriggled free and was already hurrying home. As she went, she thought about the letter claiming the Hall belonged to Olio

259

Sleevery. Had Olio written it? If so, what was he up to?

Won't be nothing good, Edie told herself. *Ought I to tell Mrs Poskett? No ... ain't nothing she can do about it.*

When Charlie and Rosie greeted her at the door – with hugs and questions – all Edie said was, "It was that Jago who rubbished your things. Sure as eggs is eggs. He ain't admitting it, though." She gave a sudden chuckle as she remembered Jago's face when he saw her. "Shut the door on me! Scared, I reckon."

Rosie giggled. "I'm not surprised! But come to the drawing room ... we're about to start the rehearsal. And we've even got curtains – Vinnie found a way to hang them across the end of the room. It looks really proper!"

"And after the rehearsal, Rosie's going to the Supper Rooms with Gertie to tell everyone we're putting on a show tomorrow night," Charlie said. "It'll be free, with a collection afterwards." He pointed to his black eye and swollen nose. "Pa says I've got to stay here. He says I look a fright and I'll scare people! But he and Aunt Mags are going to go and change the posters, and Vinnie and Mrs Poskett are going to write out some more flyers ... it's our last chance to get enough money to go home."

"And see Ma!" Rosie's eyes shone.

Edie's heart lurched at the thought of losing her friends, but all she said was, "Can I help?"

"Of course," Rosie told her, but before she could say in which way Edie could be useful there was a loud bellow from Pa.

"Charlie? Rosie? Time to begin!"

Rosie grabbed Edie's hand. "Come on! Come and see your first ever play!" And they hurried down the hallway.

Twenty-eight

CONSTABLE GRIMSHAW STEPPED UP TO THE front door of the Supper Rooms and gave an authoritative knock.

Mrs Moore opened the door. "Yes?"

"I've a gentleman out here with a complaint," the constable told her. "Lost the contents of his wallet here last night. Suspects the lady sitting next to him: green velvet dress, paisley shawl, large reticule. *Ahem*. Sounds like the magician's mother, if I may be so bold as to mention it."

This was a realisation of Mrs Moore's worst fears and she cursed herself for her greed. How could she have been so foolish as to let Mrs Snicket stay? After a nervous glance to left and right, she drew the constable into the house.

"I knew she was a thief!" she hissed. "I knew it! She shan't stay here another minute ... she's in there!" And she pointed to the parlour.

The constable thanked her with a nod – but when he opened the door, the parlour was empty.

Mrs Moore gave a scream of fury and ran up the stairs as she had never run before. On opening the door to Mrs Snicket's room, she saw clothes tumbled everywhere ... but the suitcases were gone. Hurrying to the window she looked out.

"There they go! I can see them!"

Constable Grimshaw followed her gaze. "Admission of guilt by flight," he remarked with an air of satisfaction. "They'll be headed for the station... I'll need to take some details, Missus."

"Aren't you going to go after them?" Mrs Moore wanted to know.

"I'll be bringing in the full force of the law." The constable folded his arms. "Don't you fret, Ma'am. There'll be a description out: our boys will be watching and waiting, even as far away as York."

Mrs Moore collapsed on a chair. "Evil! That's what she was, evil! And that dreadful, dreadful boy..."

Once Constable Grimshaw had taken details from both Mrs Moore and the agent from the North Western Railway Company, he took himself off to write up his report.

Mrs Moore, after some reflection, began to feel a little more cheerful. After all, she still had her iron safe, and it was comfortably full. "I'll send Jago with a message to Uncaster Hall. Miss Gertrude Gracegirdle can fill in tonight. I was going to ask her for next week, anyway. People expecting magic will be disappointed, but I can't help that."

But Jago was nowhere to be found.

Had Mrs Moore thought to look in the supper room, she would have seen Jago hurriedly packing up Baby's equipment. Five minutes later, bent double under the weight of the black box, he was at the customers' entrance checking the high street.

A heavy travelling carriage drawn by four

chestnut horses held him back for a moment, then the road was clear. Puffing and panting, he made his way towards the station, grinning a weasel's grin as he went.

"Running away! Dearie me … but nice kind Jago is bringing Baby his box of magic tricks. They'll owe me!And I'll make 'em pay!"

The long echoing sound of a train whistle broke into his thoughts, and he began to run. Enquiries at the ticket office told him what he needed to know, and with a third class ticket in his pocket he was just in time to take his seat on the train for the North.

At the other end of the train, Eliza Snicket and her son were comfortably settled in a first class carriage.

"York will be wonderful, Baby darling," she said. "Wonderful!"

Baby shrugged. "Anywhere's better than here."

"We'll never come back again," his mother promised – and her eyes gleamed as she noticed the gold pocket watch hanging from the waist of the elegant passenger opposite.

♦ ♦ ♦

A kitchen boy, clutching a hastily scrawled note from Mrs Moore, panted his way up the steps to Uncaster Hall. It was Gertie who answered his knock. She read the note, and told him the answer was yes: Miss Gracegirdle would be happy to perform.

Returning to the rehearsal, Gertie found Pa ranting on the blasted heath – a heath represented by a couple of tubs filled with branches cut from a hawthorn bush – and Vinnie, who was playing the part of a blasted oak tree.

Rosie was arranged artistically on a faded green rug at Vinnie's feet, waiting for her royal father to complete his speech so that they could sing their final song. Edie, breathless with excitement, was watching from the front row. Charlie was beside her; Gertie noticed his arm was along the back of Edie's chair, and she smiled to herself as she sat down beside Aunt Mags. Arabella was seated at the piano, poised to play.

Pa finished his rant and then, having thoroughly enjoyed himself, began his speech for a second time. Rosie rolled her eyes and sat up. "Come on, Pa, I want to practise my song!"

The noble Lear shook his finger at her. "Patience, my child, patience!" He took a deep breath. "'Blow, winds, and crack your cheeks—'" And he was off again.

Edie was fascinated. When Rosie sang her last song, Arabella accompanying her on the piano, she almost forgot to breathe and her eyes were like stars.

"That was just the most beautifullest thing I ever heard," she said, with an ecstatic sigh. "If you don't get a cap full of shiny shilling pieces tomorrow, I'll – I'll eat my boots."

Her pleasure made the company's spirits rise a little. "Will you take the hat round at the end of the show tomorrow, Edie?" Charlie asked. "You brought us lots of luck last time."

Thrilled, Edie agreed. She was equally pleased when Rosie asked her to come with her and Gertie.

"We might need you to protect us from Jago," Rosie said, and she was only half-joking.

Gertie snorted. "He'd better not try anything while I'm there, or he'll feel the back of my hand!"

♦ ♦ ♦

But when they reached the Supper Rooms, they found there was nothing to fear. The youngest kitchen boy, wide-eyed, met them at the door.

"You've got to go straight to the stage, Miss! Mrs Moore, she's in a right old state... Jago's vanished, and so has that magician and his Ma. The kitchen's in a tizzy 'cos the suppers aren't cooked, and we're jam-packed full of customers!" He gave Edie an imploring look. "Don't suppose you could give us a hand?"

Gertie hurried in the direction of the stage. Edie hesitated and then, followed by Rosie, made her way to the kitchen. There they found the cook, red-faced and sweating, trying his best to do the job of three people.

Helping herself to an apron, Edie began to peel the heap of potatoes, while Rosie tackled the cabbage. Between them, with help from the kitchen boys, the various different courses were sent out. Some dishes were charred, and others undercooked – but as Edie said, "At least it's food!"

As Rosie slopped the twentieth Swiss cream onto a dish, they heard the sound of cheering coming from the supper room and a moment later a weary Mrs Moore appeared. "Thank you for your help, girls, but you can go now. I'm closing as soon as dessert's done and I won't be opening again until Tuesday."

Edie was surprised. "Don't you do Saturdays, then?"

"I certainly do." Mrs Moore frowned. "But Miss Gracegirdle took it upon herself to announce that there's some show or other at Uncaster Hall tomorrow, and she hasn't time to sing here." She sighed heavily. "And I'm tired. It's been a *terrible* week."

Pa was spinning with excitement when he heard that the Supper Rooms were to be closed the following evening. Aunt Mags was less thrilled; she still doubted that Uncaster Hall would be a draw. It wasn't on the main street and families might well consider it had a forbidding air.

"We will triumph," Pa declared. "We will rise like ... what was that bird again? The one that rose from the flames?"

"A phoenix?" Arabella suggested.

"And so, my friends, shall we be a phoenix." Pa raised his eyes to the heavens. "We have been given one last chance, and taking it reverently yet eagerly in both hands we will—"

"That's enough, Fred," Aunt Mags snapped. "You can cluck like a chicken or rise like a phoenix, or do whatever you like in the morning, but now it's time for sleep. I'm tired." And she shooed everyone away to bed as if she herself was a skinny mother hen.

Twenty-nine

THE NEXT DAY WAS A WHIRL OF ACTIVITY. Vinnie, finding several sticks of charcoal and a pot of red paint in a cupboard, had another of his ideas. He begged for one of Arabella's old sheets, and he and Charlie created an enormous banner announcing that a spectacular, extraordinary and fantastical performance of *King Lear* was to take place that very evening in the noble surroundings of Uncaster Hall.

They borrowed two clothes poles to hold up the banner, and Vinnie and Gertie set off to parade up and down Uncaster high street, with Charlie and Rosie running ahead handing out flyers. Aunt Mags and Pa followed behind them, ready to explain what was happening to anyone who showed interest.

◆ ◆ ◆

Arabella and Edie were in the kitchen when there was a loud knocking. Almost certain she knew who it was, Arabella sighed.

"Shall I go, Ma'am?" Edie asked, but Arabella shook her head.

"You wait here, Edie dear," she said, and went to open the door.

Sure enough, Olio Sleevery was leering at her. "Made up your mind?" he asked. "Time's running out. Twelve o'clock tonight!" He gave a snickering laugh. "Cinderella without a prince. Only a pumpkin! Ha!" And then, before Arabella could stop him, he had slipped past her and was striding down the hallway as if he already owned it.

"Mr Sleevery!" Arabella ran after him. "I must ask you to leave! This is my home!"

Olio Sleevery took no notice. He had taken a small notebook from his pocket and was taking notes of the furniture. Swinging into the drawing room, he stopped in surprise when he saw the arrangement of the chairs and the curtains closing off the temporary stage area.

"What's this?" he demanded. "Playing games?"

Arabella was white with anger. "I would like you to leave at once! Uncaster Hall is my home!"

"Not for much longer." Olio Sleevery licked his lips. "Make sure you don't cheat me. You can take your clothes, but everything else is mine. Do you understand? Pots, pans, pictures. Don't you dare take so much as a pepper pot, or I'll charge you. The law's on my side. Four hundred pounds you owe me. Four hundred pounds!"

He made a tour of the rest of the room, then glanced through the doorways of Arabella's parlour, and Henry's dusty study. The dining room had him writing again; when he asked about the absence of any silver cutlery, Arabella found a certain amount of pleasure in informing him it had been stolen. He wasn't interested in the kitchen, or the rooms upstairs – putting his notebook carefully in his pocket, he got ready to leave.

"I'll give you three days to pack and get out. Make sure you take that theatre rabble with you." And with a reptilian smile, he strode up the hallway and out of the door.

Arabella shuddered. She felt as if everything around her was tainted with something sour and rotten. Seizing the broom, she began sweeping furiously – as if to clean away all memory of her visitor.

Edie came hurrying out of the kitchen. "Oh, Mrs Poskett!" There were tears in her eyes. "What are you going to do?"

"I don't know." There was defeat in Arabella's slumped shoulders. "I suppose Aunt Jocasta might still help – but surely she would have answered my letter by now."

"I says, never say die 'til you're six foot under, Ma'am."

Arabella managed a smile. "Quite right. Now, why don't you run along and join Charlie and Rosie? There's nothing more you can do here until tonight ... and they'll be missing you."

"Thank you, Ma'am." Edie looked anxious. "But what if that man comes back?"

"He won't be back so soon." Arabella picked up Edie's shawl and handed it to her. "Here you are."

A breeze was getting up as Edie walked briskly past the Post Office. It caught her shawl and floated it to the side of the road, where it snagged on an overhanging branch. As she disentangled it her eye was caught by a scrumpled piece of paper, half-hidden in the long grass; with a shock, she recognized Arabella's looping handwriting.

Picking it up, she realised what it was. "The letter to her aunt!" Edie's heart began to beat faster. "But what's it doing here?" She smoothed the paper, and turned it over. "'The Honourable Jocasta Poskett, Horsefall Towers, Little Wickham.' Oh! Oh … my poor dear lady! She'll never get no money now..." She stood still, considering. "What should I do? There ain't much time … it'd take too long to find Charlie and Rosie..." Then, tying her shawl tightly round her shoulders, she made her decision. "I'll have to help her out. Little Wickham ain't that far."

With a determined step, she set off in the direction of Horsefall Towers.

Twenty-nine

CHARLIE AND ROSIE, WANDERING UP THE high street handing out their advertising flyers, were surprised to find how many people wanted to talk to them.

The news of Little Baby Bubbles' sudden departure had spread like wildfire – the worthy inhabitants of Uncaster were split between those who believed theft and deception were no more than could be expected of any kind of entertainer who came from London, and those who were shocked but willing to consider something new. There were also thrilling rumours about Jago's disappearance: the general opinion was that he had run away with Mrs Snicket and she was going to train him as a pickpocket.

With all this extraordinary news flying

from shop to shop and customer to customer, Uncaster was unusually awake for a Saturday morning and many unnecessary shopping expeditions were taking place, just so that gossip could be exchanged in excited whispers.

In amongst the wild speculation there was a certain amount of sympathy for the Steam Whistle Theatre Company and their arbitrary dismissal from The Golden Lion. George was not popular and as it gradually became known that he was blaming the players for damage to their own property, the sympathy grew.

Miss Twillfit hurried out of her shop to ask Rosie for details. When she heard what had happened, and why the company had had to move to Uncaster Hall, her round red cheeks grew even redder. "You poor little ducks! What a crying shame! And you're putting on your show for free, you say?"

Rosie nodded but Charlie said, "We'll be taking a hat round at the end."

"Quite right too." Miss Twillfit said approvingly. "Now, my sister and I, we were thinking of taking a supper at Mrs Moore's tonight and seeing a bit of magic – but seeing as the magician's done a runner with his no-good mother, there's no chance of that. I'll tell you what! We'll come and see you instead. And my friend from the pharmacy, she and her hubby were going to come with us. So there you are... Save us four front-row seats!" And she bounced back to her shop.

"There!" Rosie beamed, but then her expression changed. "I wish Edie was here."

"Maybe she'll come after she's finished helping Mrs Poskett," Charlie said hopefully.

When Vinnie and Gertie appeared with their banner ten minutes later, opinion had definitely swung in their favour – and there were even a few cheers as they marched up and down. The usual trail of small boys and girls ran behind them, but they were laughing instead of calling names. Charlie started joking with them and Vinnie joined in. As the numbers grew, Gertie began to sing: "We're the Steam Whistle Companeee... We're the ones you want to see!" Before long, the crowd were singing too.

Pa and Aunt Mags, emerging from a side road, found themselves faced with a procession of dancing children – and Pa's smile spread from ear to ear.

"We'll do it, Mags," he said. "You wait and see! We'll be the toast of Uncaster!"

"But then what?" his sister asked. "We can't stay here. You heard what Mrs Poskett said ... she's got to sell the Hall to pay her debts."

"Tomorrow is another day." Pa took her arm. "Let's see what happens tonight! London, York, Edinburgh – the world will be our oyster! My bones tell me success is just around the corner."

Her brother's bones were notoriously unreliable, but Aunt Mags decided there was no point in arguing.

Pa was following his own thoughts. "More chairs. We'll need more chairs! Tonight, dear sister, we will play to a full house!"

Edie walked steadily along the road. After an hour or so her boots began to rub painfully, but she took no notice until a farm cart rattled up behind her.

She waved at the carter and he pulled his large hairy horse to a halt. "Want a lift, Miss?"

"Going anywhere near Little Wickham?"

Edie asked, and when the old man nodded she climbed up with a sigh of relief.

It wasn't much quicker than walking, but it saved her feet ... and gave her time to think. What would Charlie and Rosie say when they found her gone? What would happen if Aunt Jocasta refused to see her? And what would happen to Arabella and Uncaster Hall if Olio Sleevery got his way?

The hairy horse lumbered on. Edie dozed a little, looked at the fields on either side, counted the cows, wondered what the sheep thought about as they cropped the grass, then dozed some more – only to wake with a start as the cart came to a stop.

"You been asleep a good couple hours, Missy," the carter told her. "Here's as far as I go. That there's Little Wickham over that way."

Edie thanked him and got down onto the dusty road. In the distance she could see a tall tower and a shining roof, and her eyes widened. "Is that Horsefall Towers?" she asked – and the carter snorted.

"Horsefall Towers it is: wealthy old woman lives there. Won't have nothing to do with the likes of you, Missy." And he cracked his whip and drove away.

Dusting down her skirts, Edie took a deep breath. *She can't do nothing to me*, she told herself. *Talk's free.* Holding Arabella's letter as if it were a talisman, she trudged on.

The sound of horses' hooves made her look round; a smart carriage was rattling towards her, drawn by four gleaming black horses. As it passed, Edie caught a glimpse of a hawklike nose – and a shiver ran down her spine as she saw the horses turn into the wide driveway ahead.

Come on, Edie Boiler! She gave herself a mental shake. *Nobody never got nothing done by dilly-dallying!*

A smartly dressed groom was opening the carriage door as Edie walked through the imposing gates, and she hurried forward. As she did so a small terrier, barking wildly, jumped to the ground and headed for the road. Without thinking what she was doing, Edie swooped down and caught her.

"Affogato!" The voice was angry. "Could you not hold on to Pipsi for even five minutes? She'll be running away again!"

"She bit me, Auntie." Affogato sounded surprisingly subdued.

"That's no excuse! No excuse at all! Now, get out and catch her!"

As Affogato stumbled out of the coach, Edie came to stand by the door. Pipsi, seeing Affogato, began to growl, and Edie stroked the little dog's head to quieten her.

Aunt Jocasta peered out from inside the coach and her eyebrows rose. "Ha! So you've caught my dog! Give her to me."

Pipsi, however, had other ideas. She was licking Edie's arm and behaving as if she had finally found her long-lost owner; when Aunt Jocasta stretched out an imperious hand, Pipsi growled again.

"*Sh*," Edie told her. "That ain't good manners."

"Do I know you, girl?" Aunt Jocasta's eyes were cold.

"No Ma'am." Edie bobbed a curtsey with some difficulty; Pipsi was now trying to lick her face. "I work for Mrs Poskett, Ma'am ... and I brung you a letter."

The Honourable Jocasta froze. "I don't wish to read it."

Edie took a deep breath. "Ma'am, if you please, my Lady's in trouble. If you won't read the letter, I'll try and tell you – but I ain't got the proper words. It's just like Rosie says in that play, 'I can't go heaving my heart into my mouth.' But my Lady, she—"

"Just a minute!" Edie was interrupted by Hypatia, squashed in a corner of the carriage. "I know who you are! You're that scrubby little workhouse girl who lives in our kitchen—"

"Be quiet, Hypatia!" Aunt Jocasta snapped. She looked curiously at Edie. "You were quoting Cordelia. How does a girl like you know Shakespeare?"

"It's the Steam Whistle Theatre Company, Ma'am. They're my Lady's lodgers... Oh, she's trying ever so ever so hard to pay her debts, Ma'am! If you knew how hard she works ... and there's this man trying to take it all away. And I heard him talking as if Uncaster Hall was his, done and dusted, and it ain't – not yet – and she's worritted to bits—"

"Lodgers?" Hypatia's voice was a horrified screech.

"Yes, lodgers!" Edie's face was flushed. "My

283

Lady, she's working her fingers to the bone! She ain't used to it, neither – not like me – but she don't let that stop her!"

Hypatia sneered. "What do you know about anything, workhouse girl? Work's for little slave-y girls like you—"

"Hypatia! I told you to be quiet!" The Honourable Jocasta Poskett held up an imperious hand. "Get out of the carriage ... and you, child, get in. I want to talk to you."

Hypatia gasped. "But, Auntie! She's a dirty little kitchen maid!"

"And far more interesting than you, Hypatia!" Aunt Jocasta folded her arms. "Even my dog prefers her. Now, child. Tell me why you're here and what you want..."

Thirty-one

To Aunt Mags' astonishment, Pa was right: Uncaster liked a Saturday night outing and free entertainment was especially attractive. The chance of looking round a grand house was an added incentive, and as soon as it became known that respectable traders like Miss Twillfit were planning to attend there was a rush to eat an early meal before setting off for Uncaster Hall.

The company had worked hard to prepare the drawing room. The windows were shuttered, but the darkness was broken by oil lamps placed on each window ledge; they glowed golden, making the shadows deeper and more mysterious. The garden had been raided, and tall vases of roses and lilies stood in each corner, sweetening the air and glimmering pale in the gloom. Arabella had picked armfuls of ivy, and trailed the strands from one branching candelabra to the next, before tucking bunches of moon daisies between the dark green leaves; the daisies shone in the lamplight like stars. The stage, hidden as yet by thick velvet curtains, was lit by candles of all shapes and sizes in pots, teacups, jugs and jars.

Vinnie welcomed the visitors at the door and as the families tentatively made their way to the drawing room Arabella, seated at the piano, began to play a selection of simple songs and tunes. Miss Twillfit's sister, who was one of the first to arrive, seated herself in the front row and looked round before elbowing her neighbour.

"Very nice," she said in a loud voice. "A bit gloomy, but I'm thinking that's what they call 'theatrical'."

Charlie, hidden behind the curtain, peeked through a hole to see if he could see any sign of Edie. He and Rosie had been worrying about her; where could she be? Where had she gone? Surely she wasn't going to miss their first performance?

Pa, resplendent in his royal robes, put a hand on his son's shoulder. "'I am to wait, though waiting so be hell,'" he quoted. "She's part of the family, dear boy. She'll be back."

By eight o'clock there were very few empty seats left, and Arabella stood up to curtsey to the audience as instructed earlier by Pa. A round of enthusiastic applause made her curtsey a second time, and as she did so she was almost certain she could see the tall spidery figure of Olio Sleevery slipping into the darkness at the back of the room.

Settling herself once more at the piano she found her hands were trembling: what could he want? Was he going to claim the Hall in front of everyone and declare her homeless? She bent over the piano keys, trying to concentrate on the music.

The curtains swung open and there was a sharp intake of breath. Anyone well acquainted with the tragedy of *King Lear* might have wondered at the opening scene, but the Uncaster audience were dazzled. Pa, Aunt Mags and Gertie swept onto the stage, the candlelight made the artificial diamonds, rubies and emeralds on the costumes glitter as if they were real, and Regan and Goneril launched into the song Pa had written for them.

Having declared their undying love ("Oh father dear, by name of Lear, how much we do adore you! We love you best, above the rest, believe us, we implore you...") they sank into deep reverential curtsies.

Miss Twillfit's sister gave a deep sigh of satisfaction. "I do like a good song," she remarked. "Never knew that Shakespeare fellow wrote music."

Rosie had been entrusted with Shakespeare's own words: when she defied her sisters, Miss Twillfit's sister shook her head in disapproval, but made no comment. As the play progressed she grew more and more involved. Charlie, as the fool, made her hoot with laughter, and when Lear was rejected by his older daughters she stood up and shouted, "You shameless hussies!" She was persuaded to sit down again by Miss Twillfit, but continued to mutter under her breath. By the time Pa began his final rant she was clutching her handkerchief and wiping her eyes.

Pa, much encouraged by this enthusiasm, ranted his very best. Even Rosie, who had heard him a hundred times, found herself near to tears. *Dear, dear Pa*, she thought. *What would I do if anything happened to him?* And her eyes filled.

As Pa finished, she sat up to sing her final song. This was the cue for music ... but nothing happened. She glanced at Arabella and saw she was frozen at the piano, staring into the audience as if she had seen a ghost.

People began to murmur and move restlessly – but then came a cascade of rippling music. Someone was whistling the tune like an evening blackbird.

Behind the stage, Charlie smiled for the first time that evening. "That's Edie! It has to be!"

Gradually the tune grew louder; Rosie joined in and the song filled the room with the grief of a daughter who had lost the father she loved. The words were nothing special, but Rosie was still thinking about how painful it would be to lose Pa, and the whistle was sweet and true.

The audience was rapt, enchanted by the moment ... and Pa, even though he had one last speech, was wise enough to throw out his arms, bow deeply and announce: "The end."

"Enough! ENOUGH!" Before the applause could begin, Olio Sleevery had jumped to his feet and was marching towards the stage. Once there, he turned to face the startled audience. "And it's more than the end. That's the last you'll see of this rabble."

"Rabble?" Pa stepped forward, swelling with affronted indignation. "And who might you be, Sir, who interrupts so rudely?"

Olio ignored him. "All of you sitting here, gawping and staring – take your last look! This place is mine now! Mine, do you hear?" He pointed to Arabella, pale and shaking by the piano. "She's nothing but a pauper. Loaded with debts!"

Pa glowered. "And given time, Sir, I have no doubt that all her debts will be paid. We poor players are much beholden to the kindness of Mrs Poskett, and we know her to be a lady of honour—"

"HONOUR?" Olio swung round to Pa, his face distorted with rage, and hissed: "You stupid man! Did honour ever pay a debt? Did honour ever pay four hundred pounds? Because that's what she owes me! *Four hundred pounds!*"

"And four hundred pounds will be paid!" The voice boomed out, echoing through the room. "The debt will be paid in full."

The Honourable Jocasta Poskett surged forward, ignoring the audience as she swept between the chairs, until she was towering over Olio Sleevery.

"You, my fine fellow, are nothing but a sneaking, conniving, dishonourable wretch – and I will not permit vermin like you to contaminate my ancestral home!"

Olio began to protest, but Aunt Jocasta shook him like a terrier shaking a rat. "Away with you! Be gone!" And she gave him such a push that he was sent reeling off the stage.

Staggering to his feet, he scurried away, muttering as he went. As he reached the doorway, the Honourable Jocasta boomed after him, "Beware, Olio Sleevery! Your attempts to defraud my family will be made public, and your name disgraced beyond all hope of reparation."

As Olio slid into the night, Jocasta turned

to Arabella. "I'll pay my brother's debts. Four hundred pounds is the correct amount, I believe."

Arabella clasped her hands. "How can I thank you?"

Aunt Jocasta shrugged. "That's all I'm willing to give. If it wasn't for Edie Boiler, I would have done nothing for you – apart from continuing the education of your rather unpleasant children. It was Edie who persuaded me you are, as the gentleman beside me said, a woman of honour who is capable of working hard enough to save Uncaster Hall."

She stepped off the stage as if about to leave, then changed her mind. Putting her hand in her reticule, she brought out a small purse, and handed it to Charlie.

"Young man, I believe I should make a contribution to your somewhat curious – but interesting – production of *King Lear*." And then, with a swirl of her voluminous skirts she sailed towards the door.

A moment later, the Honourable Jocasta Poskett was gone.

"Hurrah, hurrah, hurrah!" It was Edie

jumping up and down at the back of the room. "Hurrah for Aunt Jocasta! Hurrah for Mrs Poskett! Hurrah for the Steam Whistle Theatre Company!"

The audience, who had been open-mouthed and staring, erupted; they cheered and stamped, and cheered again. Snatching up a hat, Edie took up her position by the door.

"Ladies and gents! We thank you for coming – now, show us your appreciation! Pennies! Halfpennies! Even a farthing if you ain't got nothing else!"

"Here, Edie!" Charlie came running to join Edie. Opening the purse he poured the contents into the hat ... seven gold sovereigns.

"Gold!" Edie was breathless. "Charlie – it's gold!"

Before Charlie could say anything the audience began to flood out of the room, fishing in their pockets for change.

"Never thought I'd see anything like that," a young man said to his friend, and the friend nodded.

"Beat that magic boy by a long shot. What did he do? A few card tricks: nothing like this."

"Were a bit more than just tricks, though," the young man said, and they went out arguing – but not before they had dropped a couple of sixpences into Edie's hat.

They weren't alone. By the time the stragglers had made their way through the door, the hat was almost too heavy for her to hold, and she was fluttering with excitement.

Miss Twillfit and her sister were the last to go. "Broke my poor old heart," Miss Twillfit's sister said. "But them two hussies! Didn't they deserve a good tanning? Mercy me ... such behaviour, and their Pa a king and all." Shaking her head, she gathered up her skirts before asking, "When's they doing it again? Whenever it is, count me in. Nothing I like more than a good cry." She opened her purse, and peered inside. "Here, ducks." And she dropped another gold sovereign into the hat.

Edie, almost too astonished to speak, managed to gasp: "Thanks, Ma'am! Thanks EVER so much!"

"That's from the both of us," Miss Twillfit informed her. "It'll be a shilling next time – and all the times after. But my word ... what an evening! *What* an evening!"

Clutching the hat, Edie walked carefully towards the stage where the Steam Whistle Theatre Company was waiting for her.

"Here you are," she said as she handed the hat to Rosie. "You can go home now." She paused, hoping her voice wouldn't wobble. "Home to your Ma."

But Arabella heard the shake in Edie's voice, and she ran forward to take her hand. "Edie! Dearest Edie! Don't you understand? You've saved my home – OUR home – and everyone can stay!"

Rosie beamed at Edie. "So we don't need to go back to London!" She was glowing. "And there's plenty to pay for Ma and the little ones to come and join us."

Charlie picked Edie up and swung her round in a mammoth hug. "And it's all thanks to you, Edie Boiler! It's all thanks to you!"

Thirty-two

THE STEAM WHISTLE THEATRE COMPANY
went from strength to strength.

Arabella Poskett became their manager,
and very soon the Uncaster Hall Theatre was
paying its way. The company became highly
celebrated – especially for the wonderful costumes made by their very own seamstress,
Miss Twillfit – and theatre impresarios came
begging them to perform in Edinburgh and
London.

Pa, however, refused to travel further than
a two-hour train journey. Uncaster, he said,
had recognized the glories of his work, and
he wasn't going too far away. He, Ma, Charlie,
Rosie and all the little ones were extremely
comfortable ... and besides, as Pa announced at

regular intervals, the North *truly* appreciated Shakespeare.

Ma took over the day-to-day running of the Hall; she had great pleasure in paying off all the landladies and landlords she had owed for years because, as she said, she was now a land-lady herself.

Vinnie and Gertie became ardent readers of the newspaper, especially the columns dealing with the convictions of petty criminals – and an item detailing the five year sentence for a certain Mrs Snicket gave them much pleasure.

Little Baby Bubbles was not mentioned, but one Horace Snicket was strongly suspected of making his living by cheating at cards ... as was his accomplice: one Jago Wilson.

A few weeks after the famous performance of *King Lear*, two weary figures appeared at the Hall and begged to be taken in: Affogato and Hypatia had had enough of Aunt Jocasta.

They were not entirely reformed, but they were so terrified of being sent back to their aunt that they behaved quite reasonably. Affoga-to became a more than adequate cook, with

Hypatia as his able assistant. Aunt Jocasta never visited again, and when she died a few years later she left her immense fortune to a charity ... a charity for retired Shakespearean actors.

And Charlie, Rosie and Edie?

They stayed the very best of friends ... and in Charlie and Edie's case, more than friends. Rosie danced at their wedding, and she and the bride both wore scarlet ribbons in their hair. Pa made the longest speech ever suffered on such an occasion, and managed to include twenty seven quotations from the noble Bard.

Only the arrival of the huge wedding cake silenced him, and even then Rosie had to beg him to be quiet.

"Food," he said with a grandiloquent sweep of his arm. "Food, and music, and love. Love is all, dear friends! As our glorious bard would have it, 'Give me excess of it!'"

Aunt Mags snorted. "Be quiet, Fred, and eat your cake."

And, for once, Pa did as he was told.

VIVIAN FRENCH has written more than 300 books for children. Her recent work includes a junior fiction series with Marta Kissi – *The Adventures of Alfie Onion*, *The Cherry Pie Princess* and *Tom & Tallulah and the Witches' Feast* – and the critically acclaimed picture book *The Most Wonderful Thing in the World*, illustrated by Angela Barrett. Vivian teaches at Edinburgh College of Art and can be seen at festivals all over the country. She helped to found the mentoring scheme Picture Hooks for aspiring young illustrators, and in 2016 she was awarded the MBE for services to literature, literacy, illustration and the arts.

Follow Vivian on Twitter under the handle **@fivekingdoms**, or visit her at her website: **www.vivianfrench.com**

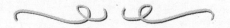